N

and

Murder

at the

Grand Island Hotel

Jennifer Branch

Dedicated to my husband, Roger Luallen,
who showed me the beauty of the
Georgia Sea Islands.

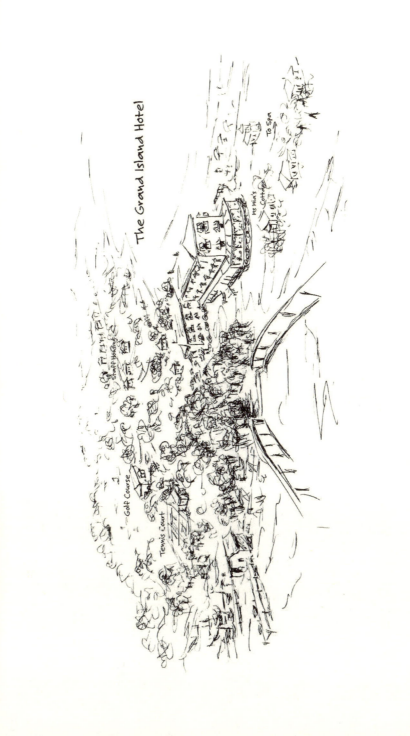

The Grand Island Hotel

Golf Course

Tennis Court

Staff Housing

Ms Mia's Cottage

To Spa

Welcome Home

Billy pulled up to the airport sidewalk in the hotel limousine and grinned at the mountain of luggage. Ms. Mia had brought everything with her, as usual. He held out his hand to the small woman beside the luggage tower, "Good to see you, Ms. Mia."

"It's been a few months, Billy. It's good to see you too." She got into the car with only her handbag, confident Billy would handle the luggage. She relaxed into the leather seat, patiently waiting for her driver.

The elderly driver took his time carefully placing each piece into the trunk, then swung into the driver's seat. "Have a nice flight?"

"Yes, thanks," Mia smiled at him in the mirror. "So, how are things? Are the kids doing well?"

"And their kids too. Five grandkids and the next on the way," he sighed. "I think the kids turned my hair gray." He smoothed his silvery crop, then propped his elbow on the window frame.

"Nonsense, Billy, my kids are grown and my hair's not gray." She patted the defiantly blond strands and laughed. "I know Jolie is having the time of her life."

"She is indeed. Never seen so many kids running through the house," Billy told her. "And the house always smells like fresh cookies." He grinned, his network of wrinkles mapping his face. "I even get to some before the grandkids."

"Just a few?"

"Well, you know," Billy patted his stomach.

"How's the hotel?" Mia asked him. "Any complaints?"

"About the same as usual," Billy assured her. "Guests last week complained about the menu not having enough choices. They mostly wanted stuff not in season like lowcountry boil, and you know how Chef's picky about seasonal ingredients."

"I know, but that's a classic dish people want to have when they come here." Mia pulled a tiny notebook out of her purse and made a note with her rose pink fountain pen. "Even when the closest fresh corn is from South America. Maybe Chef can modify it for the season. He could call it Spring Lowcountry Boil or something." She saw him wrinkle his nose in disgust.

"That's about it with the hotel, ma'am. Maria handles the hotel beautifully." He frowned a little, creases merging into new networks. "There's something odd about some of the guests right now, though."

"What's going on?" She cocked her head to one side.

"Well, you know Rebecca and Sam Forrest, of course?"

"Yes, she runs HR out of Atlanta," Mia smiled. "Nice girl. We've worked together a lot."

"Hardly a girl," Billy returned. "But very nice. She and her husband are supposed to be recreating their honeymoon for their anniversary. It's definitely not going well." He shook his head. "She mostly sits on the beach and reads, and he sits in the room and reads. About as miserable as a honeymoon gets. I don't think that marriage is lasting long." He sighed. "It's too bad. Nice couple. Young kids."

"Hmm," Mia said. "I'll have to find out what's going on there." She looked up. "Is that what's worrying you, Billy?"

"Well, that's not good, of course. Not with one of our own. But they're not the only people who aren't having much fun at our beautiful hotel."

"That famous writer, Harold Stone, is staying with us. His assistant's not having much fun, but I can't imagine any of his assistants ever do. So I'm not worried about her. She'll have fun when she quits and finds an employer who doesn't treat her like dirt. But he's always blowing up at the hospitality team, in public too, and seems miserable. Can't nothing make him happy."

"He's a big name," Mia tapped her pen thoughtfully. "It wouldn't be good if he badmouthed Spinel Hotels."

"No, it wouldn't." Billy agreed. "Well, there are a few others that seem like they might become a problem, but Mr. Stone is the only real trouble, I think. The rest are some nice couples having a good time, a few families, some weddings. A few people just enjoying the coast in the spring. They're mostly just having fun."

"Well, that's what we want," Mia said. "I plan to do a lot of relaxing myself this trip."

"Where are you coming from?"

"Spinel London," Mia grimaced. "I had to find a new manager. The one there came with great recommendations, but just wasn't up to our standards. It was a very long trip." She sighed, "The island always feels like coming home."

"It would, wouldn't it?" Billy said with a grin. "You were one of the first managers here. Before my time, of course. I was still in the Marines then." He had retired from the Marines years ago and had worked at several of the Spinel Hotels. This was his home base, where his very extended family lived. He called his various years working abroad, "sabbaticals." With all the grandkids, he and his wife needed them.

"Yes, and I met Leo here." Mia smiled fondly. Her husband of over thirty years had died two years ago, leaving her with happy memories, two wonderful stepsons and her daughter. They had lived in the company's hotels most of their married life except when the kids were young. They spent a few months setting up or improving a hotel, leaving when everything was perfect and moving on to the next hotel. Every day had been an exciting adventure with her husband. After his death, she tried to keep that same adventurous approach to life.

"Here's the bridge," Billy called as they drove across the metal span connecting Grand Island to the mainland. "Welcome home," he grinned at her.

"Home sweet home," Mia agreed, looking at the still green azaleas lining the main road through the island. Live oaks garlanded with Spanish moss met overhead, framing the road. A few more weeks and the azaleas would be in full bloom. Mia planned a short stay, for her, of three weeks. Then the hotel would hit high season, and she would be off to the next hotel. It was gorgeous in early spring on the Georgia coast.

The Spinel Grand Island Hotel took up the entire small island. Being just a few miles long, it wasn't really a grand island except for the name and the tremendous live oaks. But Grand was definitely the right name for the hotel. Going there felt like stepping into an older, more luxurious era. You could stay in adorable cottages or extravagant villas, play on a superb golf course and bike oyster shell paths through the palmetto palms to the beach. A huge new fishing pier was attached to one side of the island, with an attendant boat house for those who took their fishing and boating very seriously.

And there was the main hotel complex. It was a robber baron's dream come true, quite literally. Turrets and bay windows bulged out from the main facade, painted a putty white. You could stay in one of the little round tower rooms with a view encompassing the entire island. Or perhaps in one of the larger suites a few stories down with a private balcony shaded by gaily

5

striped awnings and a sweeping view of the seashore. There were no small rooms at the Spinel Grand Island Hotel.

Mia smiled at her first sight of the extravagant building. Large columned porches wrapped the building. Rocking chairs with plump cushions sat easy on the porches and great ferns hung from the high haint blue ceilings. Ceiling fans lazily turned, making sure there was always a faint breeze. It was good to be back.

"I'm not sure where they've put me this time, Billy."

"You're in Rose Cottage this trip, ma'am. It was redone about a month ago so it'll be nice, and you can help to polish off any rough edges. Where do you want to go first?"

"Oh, the main building as usual. Can you please drop my bags off at the cottage?"

"No problem. I'll see you around, Ms. Mia."

Billy drove off, leaving Mia standing outside the big double doors which were promptly opened for her.

"Mrs. Spinel," the young man greeted her with slick enthusiasm. "I'm so glad you've arrived. The driver's taken your luggage to Rose Cottage?"

"Oh yes, Billy has taken care of it." Mia looked around the lobby. It was set up as an old grand hotel, lots of conversation areas and a concierge desk to the side that actually was an antique. Huge French doors swung out onto the porches, bringing a sea breeze inside in good weather. The hotel felt like staying in a very expensive private house in the roaring twenties, which was what the core of the house had been before it became a hotel.

She loved the luxurious casualness of the big open room with the grand staircase at one end. It was a wonderful place to sit, people watch and maybe meet new friends. The small groupings of comfortable chairs encouraged conversations between strangers.

"I'm the assistant manager, Trey Sulley." He shook hands. His hand was hot and dry. He wore the Southern uniform of chinos and a not quite as classic formfitting button down shirt in a burgundy red. His dark hair was exquisitely sculpted into the latest mens style. "I'm so glad to finally meet you, Mrs. Spinel. What would you like to do first? Is there anything I can bring you?"

"I'd love a glass of sweet iced tea," She'd missed sweet tea in the past few months. Sweet iced tea was just not done in London.

Trey motioned to a waitress, "Sweet tea for Mrs. Spinel, Dorrie."

She smiled and nodded at Mia, glossy black hair swinging as she turned towards the kitchens.

"What else would you like?" Trey clearly wanted to be noticed by the boss.

"I'm going to just find a nice place to sit and relax for a bit, Trey." She nodded dismissal, and he went away, looking a little disappointed at not being able to immediately impress her.

Mia looked around and found a good vantage point to see the entire room. She settled into the tall linen wingback chair and smiled. When she arrived at a new hotel, she always spent some time just sitting in the public areas and getting a feel for the place. A few hours at different times of day in the main lounge could tell her most of what she needed to know about any hotel.

Dorrie put down a bright silver tray with a coolly sweating glass of ice tea and a fluffy biscuit on a thoughtfully placed table. "I thought you might want a little something to tide you over until dinner, Ms. Mia. I always forget whether jet lag is coming or going to England, but planes aren't fun to eat in either way."

"Thanks, Dorrie, the biscuit smells wonderful." She placed a little butter from the porcelain dish on the biscuit and breathed deeply. The first bite was as good as it smelled. Flaky and fluffy at the same time. She sighed in delight, "There's nothing like real Southern food, is there?"

"No, ma'am," the young waitress bustled away, looking pleased she'd thought to bring the biscuit.

Mia slowly finished her biscuit and sipped her ice tea, surveying the room. It was still early for people to gather for pre dinner greetings. Most people would be out biking, golfing or walking on the beach. That was why they came to the island, after all.

A few people sat around the lounge already. A red faced, overstuffed man sat solidly next to the empty fireplace talking to a limp woman overshadowed by big glasses. They were clearly arguing about some paperwork, and doing it loudly.

Mia frowned. Why argue in the lobby? She was old school enough to believe arguments, if they had to happen at all, should take place in private. She looked with concern. The man was clearly drunk.

As she watched, Dorrie went over to the couple, proffering a plate of biscuits. Smart girl, Mia thought. Get some food in the drunk.

The man grabbed the tray from her and shoved a whole biscuit in his mouth. He chewed roughly, crumbs dribbling down his shirt. He washed the biscuit down with what looked like straight bourbon.

His companion cautiously took a biscuit on a plate and broke off a small piece, eating it, but crumbling the rest of the biscuit with a thin hand. She spoke to the man, clearly trying to soothe him.

He barked at her, but seemed to calm down a little with food.

Dorrie came around to Mia. "Is there anything else you'd like, ma'am?"

"No, that was perfect." She nodded discreetly at the couple. "What's going on there?"

Dorrie said in a soft voice, facing away from the group in question, "That's Harold Stone, the writer, and his assistant, Sylvie something. He comes in every day after lunch and starts his serious drinking. She comes along so he can yell at her, from what I can see. He's supposed to be finishing a book, but I don't know when he has the time."

Mia nodded, "That's too bad. I loved his last few books." She looked at the red faced drunk. "Of course, I hadn't met the author yet."

"Put that off while you can." Dorrie hurried away on her next errand, taking Mia's empty tray.

Mia looked around at the rest of the big room. A nice looking old man sat discreetly snoozing in a cozy chair in a corner, resting up for dinner. A family with at least five kids came chattering through the lobby, carrying tennis rackets. She hoped they'd remembered to reserve enough courts. An elderly couple, dressed in sensible walking shoes with binoculars around their necks, came through on their way to dress for dinner. Birdwatchers, she thought.

An obviously honeymooning young couple walked toward the beach, hand in hand. A woman with long black hair and an expensive bathing suit wrap strolled in from the pool and paused by the reception desk for a moment.

The assistant manager, Trey, commanded the reception desk. That was a little odd for an assistant manager to be manning reception. She wondered if it was for her benefit or if they were short staffed. He smiled obsequiously, obviously interested in the attractive woman.

She was just thinking about wandering down to the beach herself when she heard a loud hail. "Mia!"

A tall young woman with brown hair and eyes to match strode briskly toward her, smiling warmly. She had on wide loose white pants, a cranberry colored top and carried a striped beach bag on her shoulder. She wasn't exactly pretty, but she glowed with health and a love of life.

"Rebecca," Mia smiled back. "Billy told me you were here on a getaway with Sam. I'm so glad to see you!"

Rebecca collapsed gracefully into the chair next to her and said in her warm honey voice, "I'm glad to see you too. It's been ages since you stopped for long in Atlanta."

"I'm just going up from reading on the beach. It's so nice to breath in the salt air and hear the waves splash." She continued, warm voice darkening, "Sam doesn't like sand in his book or he's had one client emergency or another, so he's stayed in the room most of the day. Some second honeymoon."

"You've had a nice day, though," Mia reminded her.

"Yes, I just wish Sam had been there more." Rebecca sighed, "Oh well, that's Sam."

"Husbands always have their quirks," Mia commented. Mine certainly did, she thought privately. She'd adored Leo, but no one was perfect.

"Yes, it's just supposed to be a romantic trip." Rebecca looked around the lounge discontentedly. "It's such a nice hotel, always been one of my favorites, besides the fact that it's so close to home."

Most Spinel Hotels employees chose to vacation at other hotels in the company, where they got considerable discounts in the off season. It was a much loved perk of the job, and there was considerable friendly competition about outdoing their fellow employees on a stay.

"So have a romantic dinner tonight," Mia suggested. "Pull out all the stops. Dress in something gorgeous, drink champagne. The little fancy dining room should have some soft piano music and delicious food. Or you can order room service and cover the room with roses. Pretend it really is your honeymoon."

Rebecca smiled her wide warm smile, "I will. I think Sam needs to leave the room for a little, so I'll go change

11

and drag him to the dining room." She looked hopeful. "A nice dinner together, no kids asking for stuff constantly, that should bring some romance out."

"Just relax and have fun, Rebecca. Remember it's a vacation." Mia smiled at her. "Go change and have a nice night." She stood up and stretched a little. "I'd better go change myself."

"Changing for dinner is one of the lovely things about staying in hotels, isn't it?" Rebecca swung her bright beach bag on her shoulder. "It feels wonderful to choose special clothes and have someone else make dinner for a change. I'll see you later!" She bounced away with new enthusiasm.

Mia walked over to Trey at the reception desk. "Would you send a chilled bottle of a nice champagne up to Rebecca and Sam Forrest's room?" she asked. "Pull out a few stops with a cheeseboard and a big bouquet of red roses and put it on my tab."

Trey frowned a little at the favoritism but said efficiently, "Yes, Mrs. Spinel. I'll do that right away."

"Yes, I want them to get it immediately. And make sure they have reservations in the small dining room in that quiet corner and tell them I made them."

"Yes, Mrs. Spinel, Mrs. Sotos wanted to have dinner with you at six thirty in the Grand Palmettos Dining Room if that's convenient for you?"

"I'd love to, but I'm going to take a quick nap to get over jet lag. Tell her eight o'clock would be perfect." Mia looked forward to seeing the hotel manager again.

"Yes, ma'am," Trey picked up the phone efficiently and Mia went to her cottage.

Rebecca hummed as she went up the stairs, skipping the elevator. Thank goodness Mia was here. She could be a very demanding boss, but if you did the work, it paid off. Mia also meddled in everyone's private life, which was one of the reasons her loving family loved her traveling around the world, interfering in the family hotels rather than in their love lives.

But Rebecca had reached the point where she desperately needed help in her marriage and Mia might just be it. They had two adorable but demanding kids and that certainly cut into their love life. In the past year, they'd grown distant, Sam almost pushing her away and retreating into his shell. He spent more and more time in his office, less at home. Being the new junior partner in his law firm took all of his time. She didn't think he was having an affair in the hours away from home. He had just been depressed and seemed so far away.

She'd planned this trip to rejuvenate their marriage but all it was doing was touching the sore spots. On the island, away from home, there wasn't the excuse of kids' activities or the office. There was just them, Sam and Rebecca, and they seemed like distant strangers instead of the best friends they had been. She'd escaped to the beach today because she couldn't stand the stress of being so close and feeling so distant. She'd needed a break.

She would take Mia's advice and treat tonight like a date night. Rebecca took a deep breath and opened the door to their suite. Tonight was date night and they were going to have fun, no matter what he felt like.

"Hi honey," she sang. "I'm home."

"Out here," he called from the balcony off the living room of their suite. She smiled at him, sitting in the deck chair in the waning sun and enjoying the sea air. "Did you have a nice day, dear? I saw you head for the beach, but couldn't spot you out there, even with that bright bag."

She smiled back at him, liking his lean black legs and long intelligent face. He looked in better spirits than he had when she'd left. "I walked for a bit, then camped under a palm tree. It's still pretty hot in full sun, even in March."

"Yes, I enjoyed reading on the balcony. I even took a nap. Pleasant shade and breeze." Sam was tall, like Rebecca, but without her relaxed charm. He was stiff and very precise around most people, but he used to be relaxed around her.

They smiled a little hesitantly at each other and both started to speak at the same time. There was a knock at the door.

"I'll get it," Rebecca dropped her bag and opened the door.

A white jacketed waiter wheeled in a cart with champagne nestled in an icy silver bucket and a covered tray of hor d'oeuvres. The smell of red roses filled the room. "Courtesy of Mrs. Spinel. She says you have reservations at eight o'clock in the Hammock Dining Room."

Sam came inside, "Wow, that looks good."

"I ran into Mia in the lobby. Wasn't this sweet of her?" Rebecca smiled her warm happy smile just for him and he smiled back at his wife. This was going to be a wonderful evening.

The waiter popped the cork with a muffled bang and poured their glasses, bubbles sparkling, then left. They clinked glasses. "To us," Rebecca said, and he repeated hopefully, "to us."

2

Glamour and Strife

ia loved dressing for dinner. Her cottage had a small dressing table in an alcove with very flattering lighting. She perched on the little pink stool and ran a touch of mascara on her eyelashes. She liked wearing makeup, but gave her blue eyes and skin just a bit of enhancement. She saved the color for her lips. She swept cherry red lipstick on her still full lips and smiled at herself in the mirror.

Finishing with two large blue spinel and diamond earrings, she remembered Leo, her husband. He'd always given her spinels, because of their name. He'd presented her with these for their tenth anniversary and they were gorgeous. She clasped a matching necklace around her neck and slipped into a simple deep blue dress she'd bought in Paris last year.

If Leo were alive, he'd smile and toast her, "Here's looking at you, kid." Since he wasn't, she toasted herself, sipping from a champagne flute.

She smiled, thinking of how she'd surprised Rebecca and Sam with champagne. There was nothing like champagne to make an evening go smoothly, give a bit of glamorous sparkle. Mia was going to make it her mission to fix that marriage. She remembered how hard life had seemed when Leo was gone all the time. It had taken time to settle into her new role as mother to her stepsons, with her husband absent. If they hadn't been able to get away together and relax sometimes, life then would have been much harder. It was important to take time to enjoy life. So few people practiced the art of savoring life now.

She hoped this trip to the Spinel Grand Island would be a relaxing one for her. The manager, Maria Sotos, was an old friend and usually had everything absolutely perfect. So far, everything seemed to be running well. She'd know after a week here what changes needed to be made, if any.

She touched up her bright lipstick one more time and closed the door of the cottage behind her.

The Grand Palmettos Dining Room was warm and inviting, a gorgeous glittering ballroom with crisp white tablecloths and sparkling silver candlesticks. Every surface reflected the candle light, creating a warm glow. A pianist played discreet classic music from the rear of the room on a small stage.

Chapter Two

"Mrs. Sotos will be here shortly, Ms. Mia," Bernard, the headwaiter, informed her, pulling out her chair at her usual corner table where she had a good view of the dining room. "May I bring you some appetizers and champagne to begin?"

"That would be lovely," Mia smiled at him, enjoying herself.

It really was a lovely room. The tall French doors lined two opposite sides of the room, open during the day, but now covered in rich blue velvet drapes, the same color as her dress. She looked down at her dress, pleased at the planned coordination.

Light sparkled around the room and made it seem like an intimate dining area as well as a wonderful place for a party. There seemed to be two large wedding groups here, Mia noticed. One group was herded to a private alcove just off the main dining room and the other smaller group shepherded to a large round table in the center of the room.

She liked having wedding groups at the hotel, but she always hired a separate expert wedding planner at hotels to handle the incredible planning involved. And they usually had an assistant or two during their local high season as well. In the Georgia Sea Islands, that would be April through June. It was incredible what brides and their mothers could want at the last minute - and the Spinel Grand Island delivered. Having two families and all their friends together to celebrate such an important life change was a very special event.

The headwaiter brought her a crystal glass of champagne at the perfect temperature and some small pastries to nibble on. "Is there anything else, ma'am?"

"Thank you, Bernard, this is perfect."

The elderly man she'd noticed napping in the lobby now had his family with him. No wonder he'd been asleep. Three very active boys and probably the man's daughter all talked at once to him. He'd needed a few minutes away from the crowd.

The birdwatchers had settled into a corner table, observing people instead of birds. She was in discrete black plumage, with a strand of pearls hanging low instead of her binoculars. He was in a proper grey evening suit with a bright red tie, polished ebony cane hooked over his chair arm substituting for his trekking pole. Mia met their eyes briefly, and they smiled at each other, politely curious.

Maria Sotos came hurrying across the room, dressed in an elegant black dress with a silk scarf draping her neck, giving soft pink color to her complexion.

"Mia, I'm so sorry I'm late. There was a problem with the door systems. Trey got the computers sorted out, luckily, so everything is working now." She sat down with relief. "I don't know why everything happens at once. One of the guests mislaid their laptop, but it turned out they'd left it in the lobby while they were working."

"That's fine, Maria, you know the hotel always comes first." Mia smiled in greeting. "Is everything okay now?"

"Oh yes, no problems now," Maria reassured her. "It's good to see you. I think it's been at least six months since you were here, hasn't it?"

"At least," Mia replied. "So what new dishes do you have to taste?"

"Mmm," Maria mused. "There's a lovely shrimp dish. Not quite Shrimp Étouffée, but in that direction. The chef calls it Grand Island shrimp and serves it with some of the locally grown lowcountry rice. It's just the right amount of spicy."

"That sounds perfect." Mia loved trying new dishes.

Maria motioned the headwaiter over and ordered for them. Mia watched her, smiling. Who would have thought little Maria the receptionist, with her big smile and long bouncy ponytail, would now be running the hotel? She had started working under Mia, thirty years ago. The last fifteen she had been running the hotel as manager, incredibly successfully.

Maria had kind brown eyes and hair dyed still to her youthful brunette, but now shoulder length. She'd gained some weight over the years Mia had known her, but she'd also gained a warm motherly glow. That wasn't surprising, since she had two almost grown children.

"How are the kids?" Mia asked.

"They're good, doing well in school. I'm hiring Jake to be a lifeguard at the pool this summer. Complete nepotism, of course," she dismissed the charge with a cheerful wink. "He did the county pool last year, so he's ready. Javier is so excited for him. We met when he was a lifeguard, you know, so I think he thinks Jake will find the love of his life the same way." She laughed, "I tell him lightning doesn't strike twice."

"They grow up so fast, don't they?"

"Unbelievably. How are yours?" Maria asked.

"They're good. They asked me when you're accepting that promotion and coming to work in Atlanta." They both laughed at the thought.

"Yeah, right. Leave paradise? I don't think so," Maria was happy where she was, with her family and her hotel.

They looked around the room, commenting on the diners like they had years ago together.

Maria nodded discretely at a very polished blonde who was being seated a few tables down. A younger man accompanied her, paying quite a lot of attention to his companion. He fussed over her, pulling out her chair and arranging her gauzy wrap with care around her shoulders. "She's Hannah Winley, Arthur Winley's wife. Here for a long weekend with that extremely handsome young man while her husband's on some business trip."

"The billionaire?" Mia noticed the grotesquely big diamond weighing down her thin ring finger. "I think her hair must take at least an hour to do."

"Oh yes, she never comes to breakfast. Just has it in her cottage."

Hannah Winley was very pretty in a plastic sort of way, with absolute perfection of makeup. Her low cut sequined dress was skin tight to a perfectly sculpted figure, and her chest sparkled with diamonds. She glittered in the candlelight.

"Sequins are a little much for this hotel in spring but she almost pulls them off," Mia commented. "I see Dr. Harris is still doing that nose."

Maria snorted, "You'd think women would want something no one else had. The little slope just gives it away." Her rounded face had smile crinkles around her eyes. She looked warm and happy.

"We have those two wedding parties now. One is going all out extravagance and hardly any bother. Just want things done right. Everyone's happy. That's the group in the side room." She nodded her head at them. "The other, wow, just wow. Nickel and diming everything and more trouble than three other weddings put together. If I didn't have Addie handling them, I know I'd blow my top." She smiled, "That's a job I was beyond glad to grow out of."

"I know, but weddings fill the hotel. And when everyone is happy, it's beautiful."

"Oh, I know," Maria agreed. "It's just sad when they aren't getting along. We do our best, but sometimes nothing's going to work."

"Now, I've had at least an hour of meetings with her today," Maria nodded discretely to a middle aged woman eating alone, dressed inappropriately in a long tie dye skirt with armloads of beaded bracelets.

"Why ever? Who is she?"

"Sissy Collinsworth. She runs fundraising for the Green Environmental Charity. They're planning a big fundraiser in a few months, and she's here to work out every detail." Maria emphasized, "Every single, solitary detail. I'm not totally convinced that she isn't staying as

23

long as she can to vacation while the charity foots the bill."

"Is she nickel and diming us too?"

"No, nothing but the best for her charity. But every single detail discussed minutely, ad nauseum. She's planned everything perfectly with Trey and still took hours discussing it with me. She got in a few digs about not dealing with less than managers at the other venues she's used, which I highly doubt. I think Trey must have offended her in some way, to tell the truth. He can be a bit short tempered. He needs to learn that keeping the customers happy IS the job," Maria contemplated. "Oh, well, it's a big event for the hotel, even with the charity discount."

"That writer, Harold Stone, looked like he was causing a bit of trouble?"

"Oh, he is, and then some," Maria said with feeling. "He's always blowing up at the hospitality team. It was his laptop that was mislaid earlier and did he yell about it. After all that fuss, Trey found it in the lobby, right where Mr. Stone left it."

She shook her head, "You would not believe the state his room gets into. I swear it makes the maids cry. His credit card's good for it, but it's a shame." She leaned toward Mia confidingly, "I don't think his books would get written at all except for his assistant, Sylvie. They meet every afternoon in the main lounge and discuss his book. I wish they wouldn't meet there, but I think he pulls it together a bit more in public. I doubt she'd want to be trapped in a room alone with him either. I make sure they're off to the side where the world isn't listening in," she shook her head despairingly. "Of course, a lot of guests are thrilled to see a famous writer, get him to autograph books and chat. The attention does tend to improve his mood." She pursed her lips in disgust.

"They're coming in now."

Mia and Maria watched the writer navigate, somewhat unsteadily, to a table with his assistant wispily trailing him. They sat with her back to the room and him blearily surveying it. The woman dithered over the menu and he bayed, "Steak, rare!" so loudly the entire room could hear.

Mia commented, "It's amazing how his books always hit the New York Times bestseller list. I think it's three in a row now. Really good books too."

"I know; impressive."

Their dinner arrived. Mia tasted the shrimp in its aromatic sauce, rolling it around her tastebuds. It was important that dinner should be a memorable experience at the hotel, and this was certainly delicious. "I love Chef's Grand Island Shrimp. It has a bit more depth than the typical étouffée."

"I know, he's very good."

"Chef François has been here about five years now? Is he still happy?"

"Yes, five years is when they really get creative and produce their best work, or they get bored and leave. François seems to be doing well here though," Maria savored a bite of her dish of pasta with an interesting sauce and tiny spring peas. "And his work is amazing."

Trey hurried over to their table, still dressed in his casual khakis, and greeted them. "Maria, I just want to tell you I've rebooted all the security computers, and everything is working perfectly now." He looked to Mia for approval.

"That's fine, Trey, I appreciate you letting me know." Maria nodded dismissal.

A high pitched, penetrating call of laughter rang out across the room, and everyone turned to the source of the exuberant noise. Trey stiffened, seeming to disapprove. He reluctantly left them and the dining room, hesitating a bit as if hoping to be called back to have dinner with his bosses.

The woman with long black hair she'd seen in the lobby was the source of laughter. The waitress must have said something funny because she still chortled, but much quieter than the first disruptive burst of laughter. She wore a very expensive, off the runway dress, with interesting inserts of unexpected reds into the hot pink sheath that highlighted her slim silhouette. "Who is she?" Mia motioned toward the stylish woman.

"Oh, that's Allison Jayton. She's been here a few days. Seems nice. Lots of money and a new outfit for every possible occasion. She and her partner owned a big online real estate firm, but her partner died. She sold the company for millions. She's spending as much as she can to make up for lost time. And grief too, I think."

"She has a Dr. Harris nose too."

"I know, everyone who's anyone flocks to the same doctor. It's a little ridiculous when you can spot four in a room. Who'd want a trendy nose? Allison spends a fortune in the spa too. Won't let one strand of gray show." Maria shook her brown hair. "Not that I will either."

"And I'm still a natural blonde," Mia agreed, smiling. Her hair was classically styled in a relaxed Grace Kelly bob. Not a gray would dare show in the soft ash blonde locks.

They had apple pies and ice cream for dessert. The delicate pies were a miniature version of the classic comfort food, brought to a superb level with flaky pastry and intriguing spices. They finished with satisfied sighs.

"Do you have any plans for tomorrow?"

Mia thought a minute. "I'm definitely making time for a long walk on the beach. That's one thing London was missing. Beautiful parks, but no beaches. I think I'll just wander around and absorb the hotel."

"Perfect," Maria said. "I'd love to know what you think of the tennis court renovation, if you head that way. And of course, I put you in Rose Cottage. It was just redone."

"I'd be glad to look them over," Mia made a quick note. "Anywhere else?"

"I've been wondering about an area for older kids when it's hot or raining. They get a bit cooped up on rainy summer afternoons, and it would be good to have somewhere to stash them that's not in the main areas."

"Not too far out of the way, either," Mia smiled, thinking of the trouble her step sons had managed to get in. Nothing too serious, but... "That's a good idea. I'll sleep on it." She rose, placing her linen napkin precisely beside her plate.

Maria stood with her. "Let me know if you need anything." They hugged, "It's great to see you."

They left the grand dining room and Mia walked through the soft southern night to her cottage. It was just a few steps away down a well lit sidewalk. It was pleasant walking through the huge live oak trees and seeing the long Spanish moss shimmering in the moonlight. An owl hooted far too close, and she jumped a little, laughing at herself.

She opened the cottage door, and let herself in. It had been a long day, and she was ready for bed. She changed out of her dress into a long soft pink silk nightgown, taking off her jewelry and makeup and gently patting her face with her expensive and lusciously scented serum. Her silk pillow was already placed on the turned down sheets. She laid her head on it and fell fast asleep to the distant sound of ocean waves.

Mia began the next day with a brisk walk down the beach. Walking was her primary exercise, and she loved exploring new places. This beach appeared familiar, but beaches were in a state of constant change, renewing themselves with every storm that passed. Rolling dunes backed the smooth sand beach, making it a wonderful place for long walks.

Not too many people had emerged yet this early in the morning. She nodded to a few of the wedding guests out walking before the weddings this afternoon. She passed Sissy Collinsworth walking in the surf, batik printed skirt dragging the water behind her. Allison Jayton ran by in bright running gear, her long black ponytail streaming past her like a banner.

Sam Forrest slowed from his loping jog to a walk as he passed her. "Mia, good to see you." Mia was one of the few people he was relaxed with. They'd worked together on a few lawsuits over the years, and they'd gotten to know each other well.

"And you too, Sam. I had a nice chat with Rebecca yesterday."

"Thank you for the champagne. It was very thoughtful of you and set a perfect mood. We had a wonderful dinner too." He smiled fondly.

"I'm glad," she twinkled at him. "You two need a break."

"Yes, my work has been very long hours since I made partner, and Rebecca's been bearing the brunt of childcare. She's exhausted, I know."

"You both need to have some fun. That's the point of a vacation," she urged. "Take her out on a boat today."

"You know, I think I'll do that. Rent a boat and just play," he grinned like a boy, relaxed and happy, with a fun new plan. "Nothing like messing about in boats, is there?"

"Have fun," she called as he ran in long strides back toward the main hotel, intent on his boat outing treat.

Their marriage would be all right, she thought warmly, enjoying the feel of the sand sliding under her sandals. She walked for a few more minutes, then stopped and looked out to sea. The sky looked bright and blue and the ocean endless. She breathed in the salt air. A few dolphins played in the channel, jumping in the waves. She sighed in happy appreciation.

Sam arranged a sailboat rental with the concierge, then went to tell Rebecca. He opened the bedroom door with a happy call, "Time to rise and shine, beautiful! We're going sailing!"

His wife opened her eyes and rubbed them, like a sleepy child waking, then stretched, her long tanned legs contrasting with the crisp white sheets. "Sailing?"

"Sailing," he said firmly. "It's time to really have a vacation."

"Oh, Sam," she looked at him with warm brown eyes and his heart melted.

Mia got back to her room with renewed spirit, changed to pink tennis shoes and patted her hair into sleek waves. She swiped on bright pink lipstick to match her flowing silk blouse and felt ready for the day.

Her feet padded cheerfully on the sidewalk as she headed to the Grand Palmettos Restaurant for breakfast. The morning mood was completely different in the room. Open tall windows flooded the room with bright morning light. Silver still sparkled the tables, but the candles were gone and discrete daylight lighting made the room a bright awakening. She was ushered smoothly to the same table she'd sat at last night, and she surveyed the room again.

A few of her fellow beachgoers were settling in for their well deserved breakfasts. She didn't see Sam and Rebecca. She hoped they'd had breakfast in the room, after his jog. The birdwatching couple perched at a table next to the window, bird books and map laid out between them, planning their attack. Hannah Winley wouldn't emerge for breakfast, from what Maria had said, but the handsome young man accompanying her was there, still in sweaty running clothes. She couldn't believe he hadn't bothered with a shower first.

She summoned the headwaiter and motioned to the young man. "Did you suggest breakfast in his room?"

"I suggested the terrace too, several times," the well groomed young woman sighed. "I didn't like to make a scene since he's here with Mrs. Winley. I finally just seated him as out of the way as possible." He was next to the hospitality team door.

"You did your best," Mia commiserated. "There's not much you can do when guests choose not to behave appropriately." She surveyed the wonderful menu options. "I don't think I'll experiment today. Just a plain omelette and coffee, please." She felt like comfort food, and it was always good to check the basics were up to standards.

"Right away, Ms. Mia," the headwaiter gave orders to a waitress who bustled off.

The day was going to be a lovely one, Mia thought. She'd take one of the hotel bikes on a trip around the island. The wide flat paths were perfect for leisurely bike rides, and it would be a fun way to check out the outlying areas.

Her waitress filled her cup with coffee. She added just a touch of sugar and milk, barely lightening the steaming brew. "Delicious," Mia nodded approval to the waitress, and she bustled away to fill another cup.

The waitress was new, like a lot of the less senior resort team. People would work at a hotel for a while, then move on to another hotel or job. It was a business with a lot of transient workers but senior team members did tend to stay. The only new senior employee here was Trey Sulley, the assistant manager, she thought. She might see if he was available for lunch, since she liked to get to know all the resort team.

The omelette arrived, delivered with an uncertain flourish by the waitress, who seemed to know how it would be judged. Mia approved of the simple garnish of a bit of fine herbs, but the omelette itself looked dry and rather disgusting. She took a bite to make sure. Definitely not what should be served at a Spinel Hotel.

She took the plate and walked her pink sneakers back to the kitchen, bumping through the hospitality team door. She called out in a clear voice, designed to cut through the kitchen noise, "Who cooked this?"

There was a shuffle for who was in trouble and a young man in a tall chef hat came shyly forward, "I did, Mrs. Spinel. Francisco González."

"Mr. González, did you go to culinary school?"

"Yes, of course, Mrs. Spinel. I went to Le Cordon Bleu. I did the program in Mexico City," he said with nervous pride.

She pointed to the omelette, "And they didn't teach you to make an omelette?"

"To tell you the truth, ma'am, this is the first day I've done breakfast. I usually work at night under Chef François. I did the extra Pâtisserie course so Mr. Sulley put me on for breakfast when the breakfast chef called in sick." He pointed to a gorgeous tray of croissants waiting on the counter.

"I see," Mia was disappointed, but not surprised. There were always gaps in even the most trained chef's education. "It's surprising how often they teach the showstoppers but not the basics." She looked around, "Where's an omelette pan?"

The resort team crowded around, watching the show. The young chef looked very awkward and handed her a small carbon steel frying pan. "Here, ma'am." His hands tucked in his apron.

"So, this is how you make an omelette." Mia put the pan on the hot flame. "Two eggs, please."

He handed them to her nervously, eggs juggling in his shaking hands.

She broke them into a bowl, added salt and whisked briskly. "You don't want a froth, just light and well mixed." She dropped a large pat of butter in the hot pan and moved it around. "Brown the butter lightly, then add the eggs." She did so and they started cooking as they hit the hot pan. "Now, shake like crazy." She took the pan off the stove and moved it around at a furious rate. "That creates layers in the omelette. You don't want a fluffy, dry omelette, you want a delicately layered one. When it's cooked barely enough, flip it," she tossed it up in the air and caught the eggs neatly. "Cook it just a tiny bit more, then roll it gently onto a plate, folding it into thirds as you roll." She suited her actions to her words. "Sprinkle the herbs, and you're done."

Mia displayed her perfect omelette to the restaurant team. "Try it." They clustered around, tasting spoons ready.

"That's perfect," said the young chef. "Just a few changes makes all the difference, doesn't it?"

"With eggs, little things make all the difference," Mia agreed. "So now you make me one."

He followed the steps exactly, and she had her perfect omelette. "I'll just eat while I'm here. Would you mind getting me another coffee?" she asked a waitress.

"No problem, Mrs. Spinel," her waitress brought her another perfect cup. "Where did you study for culinary?" she asked curiously.

"All over," Mia told her. "I never had time to do a full program anywhere, but I've taken classes almost every place I've lived. I actually took the Mexican Cuisine Diploma at the Cordon Bleu Institute in Mexico City while we were there for a few months opening a new hotel." She smiled as she remembered a very busy few weeks in the kitchens.

"I'm also lucky enough to get to watch all the hotel chefs at work behind the scenes. There's always so much to learn in a kitchen." She smiled at the waitress. "Whenever I'm home, which isn't often any more, I love to cook what new dishes I've found."

"Sounds like fun." The waitress hurried back to the dining room with the fresh coffee.

Mia enjoyed her omelette and lingered over her coffee, watching the kitchen. The young chef, Francisco, had the kitchen under control, and wasn't as nervous now. The omelette seemed to be a small stumbling point that a short lesson had fixed.

He offered her a still warm croissant diffidently. As the delicate flakiness melted on her tongue, she knew why he had chosen pastry as a speciality.

"That is absolutely perfect, Francisco. I haven't had a croissant that delicious outside of Paris."

He blushed and mumbled something and went back to his work. The kitchen was running beautifully. As she watched, she saw another perfect omelette go out the door, this time by a junior chef who grinned when he saw her watching. Francisco was stepping up to the challenge now and learning from a small mistake. Good, she thought.

"Thank you so much," she said to all, like a guest leaving a party.

"Bye, Mrs. Spinel, see you at lunch," they chorused, keeping to their work.

Leaving through the service door, she walked over to the side building where the bikes were stored. She checked one out from a cheerful girl in a neat blue hospitality uniform and long ponytail.

As she pedaled down the bike lane on the main drive, she looked around, planning her route. The bike was a fifties baby blue cruiser and fit well with the old fashioned atmosphere on the island. She passed the golf course on the right and waved to Billy in his limo, out to gather another group of guests.

Later she would play a round of golf to check the course, but it wasn't her favorite activity. Leo had always been the one to check those out, and now his sons made sure their golf courses were world class. They loved golf. She preferred the spa.

Live oaks met over the road, blocking out most of the sunlight with their trailing Spanish moss. A few rays of light streamed through, dancing spotlights through the shadows on the oyster shell road. She heard birds singing, getting ready for spring. She pedaled along briskly, enjoying the easy movement on the flat road.

She saw the first group of resort team cottages on her left and turned in to the little loop. They were pleasant cottages, in the same style as the rest of the hotel cottages, but a little bigger since people lived there full time.

Hospitality team in management positions lived in these if they chose to. Since sometimes they had to be on duty at odd hours, it made their lives easier.

Maria Sotos, as general manager for the hotel, had her house a little separated from the others off the next turn. At the far end of the island was some tiny apartments the junior hospitality team were generally queuing up for. An apartment within walking distance from the beach was a nice perk of the job, even if it came with occasional late nights. Any hospitality members not living on the island would have a twenty minute commute each way to the nearest town.

The cottages on this loop would be the homes of the two head chefs and assistant managers, all of whom worked late. Addie, the wedding planner, who needed to be there at unexpected hours to reassure brides, had the smallest cottage with bright red geraniums in pots next to the front door. Addie herself was heading out the door as Mia pedaled around the loop. She waved, "Hi, Ms. Mia! Good to see you! I'm off to finish the weekend's first wedding."

Mia waved, "Good luck!"

"Fingers crossed as always!" She walked briskly down a direct path to the main hotel, her high heels barely slowing her at all.

The houses on this loop seemed to be in good repair. The hotel landscapers took care of the yard maintenance, though some, like Addie, planted their own personal touches. She nodded to herself in approval. It was important to have every bit of the grounds perfect at all times. You never knew where guests would turn up. The little bike paths crisscrossing the island were meant to be used, after all. These cottages were part of the landscaping.

Trey Sulley wandered out of his little house, Allison Jayton at his side. She was still in her bright running clothes. They were walking very close and talking softly to each other. He leaned in to whisper in her ear, laughing, then released his hand from her waist. She brushed him off with a smile and waved as she followed the path Addie had taken.

Hmm, Mia thought. She wasn't at all surprised the assistant manager would have an affair with a guest. She just hoped he wouldn't do anything to cause the woman to take offense with the hotel if it ended badly.

Trey noticed Mia biking around the circle and held up a hand. "Mrs. Spinel, good to see you! How are you?" He came forward to greet her as if she'd biked directly to his house to visit.

She stopped politely, "Hello, Trey. I'm well, and you?"

"Just perfect, Mrs. Spinel." He came and held her bike's handlebar, smoothly preventing her from moving unless she rudely jerked it away.

Mia prepared herself to listen to whatever he had on his chest. "I'm so glad you came to see me, Mrs. Spinel. I knew we would get along," he smiled disarmingly at her.

"I was just out biking, Trey."

"Oh, of course, Mia," he agreed, clearly thinking it was his charming self she'd come to see. He continued to hold her bike hostage. "Such a pretty name, Mia. I could show you around the island some, if you'd like. I've worked at hotels all over the world. I have a lot of ideas for fixing this place up, trust me. I know a few places not too far away where we could have a quiet," he smiled seductively, "conversation."

Mia stiffened slightly. She disliked anyone calling her by her first name until she asked them to. She preferred to maintain that little bit of distance until she knew people well. And she was not going off anywhere alone with this particular employee. "I'm making a loop around the island so I'll just get moving." She looked determinedly at the exit to the cottage loop.

"You stay very active for a woman your age, Mia. Takes a lot to keep that figure going," he boldly looked her up and down.

Okay, that was enough. She rudely jerked the bike away and started pedaling in one smooth motion.

He didn't say anything, just laughed knowingly as she pedaled away. "Bye, Mia. I'll see you later."

What a creep, Mia thought. She couldn't believe someone as pretty as Allison Jayton would slip off to meet him. Of course, redoing your nose implied a certain lack of confidence.

She was going to have a serious talk with Maria about her creepy assistant manager choice next time she saw her. She pedaled through the dappled shadows of the main road, relaxing into the steady rhythm of the bike.

Allison hurried down the oyster shell path, not sure exactly why she was hurrying. She'd just had a nice breakfast with Trey. He wasn't a great cook, but he'd cooked for her and that was nice. And he was handsome, in a male model sort of way, dark hair and blue eyes. A handsome man cooking you breakfast wasn't a bad way to start the day.

They'd met this morning when she'd paused to stretch at the furthest point of her run. Her legs and back didn't hurt as much when she paused for a stretch midway, even on a short run. Beach runs were definitely using muscles her treadmill had not.

Trey asked her to breakfast, and, after all, she was here to start finding a new life and friends for herself. So she'd said yes.

It had been pretty obvious he'd planned to cook breakfast, then she'd smoothly tumble into bed with him. He'd held her hand and just looked at her with those devastating blue eyes and said he understood.

And she'd run away. Why?

Allison slowed her pace a little on the path, then stopped and looked at the palmetto trees all around her. Bugs made noises in the leaf litter, scritching and scratching. A bird screamed harshly over her head, making her jump. She slowly turned around in a circle, looking at the live oaks and gray Spanish moss meeting over her head, trying to spot the screeching bird. The grey green world swirled around her, making her dizzy.

After her bike ride, Mia lunched on the terrace. It was a perfect day with fluffy white clouds making their stately procession against the deep blue sky. From the terrace, she could see a few shrimp boats out in the distant water, surrounded by gulls.

As she sat enjoying her salad and the ocean view, Sissy Collinsworth came up, still in the same batik skirt she'd dragged through the sand and surf that morning. She put her hand on a chair and sat down at the same time she asked, "Mind if I join you?"

Mia nodded noncommittally. She wasn't about to cause a scene in her own hotel, and she was almost finished with her salad.

"I'm Sissy Collinsworth," the woman stated. "From the Green Environmental Charity." She shoved her dirty hand above Mia's salad.

Mia took her hand gingerly, "I'm Mia Spinel." She wiped her hand discretely on the napkin in her lap.

"Yeah, you're one of the hotel owners, aren't you?" Sissy informed her. "I've been talking with your manager about my fundraiser in three months."

"That's nice," Mia said blandly. She took a few more bites of her salad, preparing for a quick getaway.

Sissy's face shown with ardent enthusiasm. "Yeah, it's going to be a huge event. People flying from all over the world to raise money for environmental causes."

Mia thought she saw a flaw in that, but declined to say so. Her business was travel, after all.

Sissy went on, bracelets jangling, "I just feel that for so worthy a cause - I mean, you don't want the icebergs melting and flooding this place in a decade - you might give us more of a break on the cost." She looked expectantly at Mia, sure of her emotional appeal.

Mia resented Sissy interrupting her peaceful lunch in order to circumvent her managers. She went on attack in the best sweet Southern lady tradition. "Oh, my dear, are you not getting our standard charity discount? I can't believe they didn't offer that to you." She shook her head in feigned disappointment.

Sissy looked uncomfortable, shifting her weight on the chair, "Well, yes, we're getting that but.."

"Oh, that's good," Mia said brightly, "but I can't imagine giving your group more of a discount than Save our Children. I know we hold one of their major fundraisers here every year, and we always give them our charity discount. To take away from a children's charity or other worthy causes wouldn't possibly be fair, would it?" She looked at Sissy with innocent blue eyes. Mia knew perfectly well they offered the same hefty discount to all charities. It generally prevented this sort of problem.

Sissy went on offensive, "Icebergs melting will cause so much more suffering…"

"Than children starving now?" Mia said with a sniff. "I hardly think so." She stood up, placing her napkin on the table emphatically. "I can't possibly offer you a better discount than any of the other charities who hold annual fundraisers here. It just wouldn't be right." She smiled sweetly, "If you have any further questions, please talk to Trey Sulley, the assistant manager you've been working with. I'm sure he can answer any questions you have."

Sissy Collinsworth stood up and said in harsh judgment, "I can't believe you're refusing to give back to your community, to the environment."

Mia just looked at her, "Excuse me?"

"You won't give us even another percent off cost? It's for Mother Earth," she spread her arms wide, encompassing the landscape and knocking over a water glass with her floating sleeve. "Oh, sorry." A waitress hurried to clean up the broken glass.

Mia had had enough. "If you would prefer to go with a more environmentally friendly hotel, please do so. If you can find one," she added smoothly, knowing that would be extremely difficult in this area.

"Oh, well," Sissy backpedaled. "You don't even have solar panels," she accused.

Mia was abruptly sick of this woman. She felt no need to explain to Sissy that solar panels would have caused tremendous ecological damage to the island with relatively little benefit. She should know. The same eminent environmental architects had insisted on installing half a million dollars of them in their Arizona resort. She still cringed at that retrofit price tag.

She said firmly, "No, we don't." She smiled with sweet insincerity, "I do hope you enjoy your stay." She walked quickly away before Sissy could make more arrogant demands.

There was definitely a downside to people knowing you were one of the hotel owners. The discount for my very special event plea happened fairly often, but she had heard everything from "my pillow is too soft" to "I don't like the room color." She tried to politely listen. It was her family's hotel, after all, and she was here to improve it, if needed. If the complaints were valid, she wanted to know about them, but the number of people wanting special treatment for no valid reason was always annoying.

Mia decided her next stop would be the newly renovated tennis courts. That should be far enough from the terrace to avoid Sissy. She liked watching tennis a lot more than watching golf. It was fun when the players were skilled, lunging for impossible shots and sending them shooting across the court. It was almost as entertaining when they weren't so skilled and swung their racquets ineptly at open air. She smiled, thinking of her children's first tennis lessons where they whacked the ball at nothing.

She might play a game or two herself if she could find a partner. The soft grass of the courts here was a pleasure to play on.

She wandered through the locker rooms, placed thoughtfully so players could leave racquets and anything they might need at the courts and not have to carry them back and forth from the hotel.

The tennis courts backed up to the golf course so the pro shops and locker rooms flowed into each other, allowing employees to man both. She fussed with a few displays, the slightly more experienced clerk obviously telling his junior to just leave her alone. When she had the store displays looking like she wanted, she nodded to the two gawking boys hiding behind the counter. "Take care, boys."

"Yes, Ms. Mia," they chorused, grinning with relief she was going.

The newly renovated courts were gorgeous, lushly green. The precisely mown grass (eight millimeters in height) was perfectly maintained and constantly refreshed, with bright white titanium dioxide lines renewed at least daily.

Four members of a wedding party played doubles on the green courts, with one player on each side playing well and the other missing even the easiest of shots. The carefree, laughing party didn't seem to mind either way.

Hannah Winley and her handsome companion played a different sort of game. Hannah's tennis dress was fussily adorable, white with a short skirt and pink ruffled shorts showing every time she moved. Her game was not up to her youthful fashion choice.

Mia sat in the low row of stadium seats for a minute, watching. She wouldn't be surprised if the young man was a tennis pro. His game was excellent, despite his companion's ineptness.

Allison Jayton, who she'd seen coming out of Trey's house, walked over and sat near her to watch the players. She nodded at Mia, "You're Mia Spinel, one of the hotel owners, aren't you?" Mia nodded, and she leaned over to shake hands, "I'm Allison Jayton."

"Nice to meet you, Allison," Mia returned. "Are you enjoying your stay?"

"Oh yes, it's a lovely hotel," she said enthusiastically. "I'm having a wonderful time." Her gorgeous black hair swung in a sleek wave around her face.

With the woman closer and in bright sunlight, Mia could definitely see the faint signs of plastic surgery in her lightly tanned skin. She'd had not just her nose done, but pretty extensive work around her eyes and mouth. Her eye color had been changed with contacts to a very striking blue. Odd, she seemed young and pretty for such drastic changes. She much preferred changing her face with a nice spa day and relaxation.

With a start, she realized the other woman had been talking to her. She caught up the thread of conversation, "... always dreamed of coming here. It's so beautiful on the coast with all these little barrier islands. I'm even thinking of moving near here, maybe Charleston or Savannah."

"It's a lovely area," Mia agreed. "It gets very hot during the summer, but during the winter, you can continue with life instead of hiding inside." She herself liked skiing and hot chocolate too, but it was all good. "Where are you from?"

"Oh, a little town in the Midwest you've never heard of. I live in San Francisco currently, but now that I've sold my company I'd like to relocate. San Francisco's not what it used to be."

"Take time to find somewhere you really love," Mia encouraged. "Spend some time traveling and seeing the world."

"Yeah, I don't really have anywhere definite in mind, but this place is so beautiful I'm seriously thinking of it. I'm in no hurry to settle down right now." She sighed heavily, "I worked all the time the last few years, so all my friends were business friends. Then my partner and I were in this awful car wreck," she looked off into the distance, seeing the past instead of the live oaks. "I was driving. It was raining really hard. Just a stupid accident, but she died. The company just didn't seem worth doing any more without her."

"I'm so sorry," Mia said with great sympathy. "After a tragedy, sometimes it's better to make a change." No wonder Allison had had all the plastic surgery after a bad car wreck. That was what plastic surgery was for, to help people rebuild their bodies and lives. "You need to find who you want to be next."

"Yeah," Allison looked sorrowfully across the green tennis court. "Just time to make a change." She smiled a little. "I'd always dreamed of traveling around, seeing the world. So here I am. Going to all the places I read about." She bravely smiled.

"Good for you, Allison."

They were quiet a minute, then Mia commented after a particularly amazing shot, "That young man there is very good at tennis, isn't he?"

Allison laughed her high distinctive bray of laughter, "I think he's her tennis pro. She's got to keep up her practice, you know."

"How nice," Mia said with a smile. "I guess her game is coming along."

"It should be with all that practice," Allison commented. "I think he's usually there all night." She winked sardonically at Mia and stretched. "I think I'll have a bike ride, soak in the atmosphere."

"It's a perfect place for biking."

"Nice and flat," Allison enthused. "Quite a change from California hills. I'm looking for more relaxed activities, after my accident. I used to mountain bike, rock climb, do triathlons." She rubbed her legs reflectively, "I think some nice flat biking sounds perfect."

"Absolutely. Have fun," Mia said. She watched Allison head toward the bike stand. Trey wouldn't be her choice but she supposed he was just a vacation fling. Poor girl, having her friend die in a car wreck. She was glad Allison was restarting life with a nice vacation.

Mia watched the players, the handsome young man serving directly to Hannah Winley. Despite her phenomenal figure, she wasn't in very good shape. She huffed and puffed and her elaborate makeup ran with sweat. He lobbed balls to her and it was all she could to do to return them.

Finally, Hannah held up her racquet, "That's enough, Phillip. I'm beat."

The tennis pro laughed, "You're doing great, Hannah," he encouraged. "Try a few more shots."

She whined, "I am so ready for a shower." She grabbed her matching pink bag. It had ruffles. "I'm headed back."

"Sure thing, beautiful," he said agreeably. He grabbed the bucket of balls and the basket fell over. The balls rolled across the court. "Well, damn." He stooped and grabbed. "I'll just pick these up."

"Just leave them, I want my shower," she said, annoyed. "The hospitality team will take care of it."

He went on picking up the balls, "It'll just take a minute."

She watched him impatiently, tapping her foot, then kicked a ball toward him. "Here's one."

Phillip stepped on the unexpected rolling ball, almost caught his balance, then skated on another ball with the other foot. He fell with a thud and sat up yelling. "My ankle!"

Hannah said impatiently, "I'm sure you just twisted it. Try walking it out."

He lifted his foot. The ankle was visibly swelling. "I think it's broken."

"There's no way," Hannah told him. "You just turned it a little."

Mia grabbed her phone and called the front desk, requesting help.

She ran down the stairs to the grassy court, reassuring the young man. "I called for an ambulance and ice. They'll be here soon."

"Thank God," he said, grimacing in pain.

Hannah looked pouty. "I can't believe you did that," she laughed cruelly. "You almost did a flip."

The handsome young man just looked like he was in a lot of pain.

Mia checked out the ankle, loosened his laces and gently pulled his shoe off. "We'll have the ice soon, but let's get your shoe off before we have to cut it off."

He turned green as she pulled it off and his eyes rolled up a little. "Definitely broken," he muttered.

Misty, the spa receptionist, came running with ice and a first aid kit, her smooth dark ponytail bouncing. "I'm the first aid person on duty."

Mia always had several of the resort team at each hotel trained in emergency aid. When so many out of shape hotel guests decided to do their yearly exercise all at once, it saved lives.

Misty caught sight of the ballooned ankle and her round cheeks sagged in sympathy, "Oh, wow, that looks awful."

Her sleek ponytail swung as she turned to Mia, "The ambulance will be about thirty minutes, Ms. Mia. I'll just keep it elevated and iced until then."

She turned efficiently to Phillip, "Do you want Tylenol now or hold out for the good stuff with the EMTs?".

"I think Tylenol now," Phillip said through clenched teeth. "It's pretty bad."

Misty grabbed the medicine and elevated his foot. He winced as she gently placed an ice pack on the ankle already swollen to twice normal size.

"Oh, sweetie, I'm so sorry," Hannah told him, finally seeming to realize he was actually hurt. She still seemed impatient with the fuss he was creating.

"Don't worry, the hospital here is very good," Mia reassured him.

The ambulance arrived shortly and the EMT's efficiently loaded Phillip in the ambulance, Hannah remaining behind. He didn't seem to care, relaxing into their professional care with relief. Before the ambulance was out of sight, Hannah had headed back to the hotel.

Misty commented, "Wow, she's cold." She waved the ice pack and ran, "Everyone's coming to the spa today. Gotta go!"

The boys from the pro shop had gathered up most of the scattered balls. She grabbed one more and threw it in the bucket. "No more accidents today."

"I sure hope not," they both agreed fervently.

She started walking to the hotel to dress for dinner. The warm air was cooling into evening.

Mia ran into Rebecca and Sam coming back from the dock. Their hands were entwined, and they were laughing. Mia was going to leave them to their fun, but they called in unison, "Hi, Mia!"

50

"Did you enjoy the boat?"

They grinned. Rebecca's face was alive with happiness. "What a great day! We took out one of the little sailboats and just played around."

"Just the right amount of wind," Sam enthused.

"That's right, you used to sail when you were a kid," Mia remembered. "Did it bring back memories?"

"Absolutely, but it made better ones," he smiled at Rebecca, his eyes sparkling and she blushed.

"I'm so glad you're having a good vacation."

"A great vacation," Sam said, swinging Rebecca around. She laughed in delight.

"Bye, Mia," Rebecca called as they ran off hand in hand.

Mia smiled. That couple had just needed a break. She loved the freedom hotels gave people to relax from the worries of regular life. Everyday worries melted away for a few days and became easier to deal with when they returned home. She walked slowly on, letting the young couple get far ahead of her.

As she passed Harold Stone on the path, he called out peremptorily, "Hey, you!"

Mia slowed, but didn't stop. She generally did not answer to "you." He yelled again, "You! Spinel. You own this shit hole, don't you?"

She stopped abruptly and turned, "Excuse me?"

"You own this place, right?" He backed slightly down at her icy glare.

"I do," she cooly stated.

This early in the evening, he was already too drunk to communicate clearly. "Well, I have a complaint to make!" He put his Scotch infused face way too close to hers, using his height and girth to intimidate her.

"Indeed." Mia stood her ground against his fetid breath.

"About your manager," he heeled to one side of the path, then recovered balance.

"Yes?"

"He's been stealing from me."

"My manager is a woman," Mia told him.

"No, that skinny runt with the slick hair. The thief. He stole my laptop," he accused blearily.

"Ah, your laptop," Mia tried to remember. "It was found in the lobby, correct?"

"He put it there," Harold Stone charged.

Mia had a policy to never argue with drunks. "I'll have to look into that," she pacified him.

He swayed up close to her again with his heavy breath. "I'll sue."

"I'm sure there's been some mistake."

He leaned in, blustering, "You can't steal from me."

Mia thankfully saw Billy hurrying up the path toward them. "I'm sure there's been some mistake, but I will look into the incident."

The small man gently but firmly took hold of Harold Stone's arm, "Can I help you back to the hotel, sir." It was not a question. His sinewy arm was pure muscle.

The heavier man struggled in Billy's seemingly light grip but couldn't get away. Billy smoothly said, "You don't seem to be feeling well, sir. I'll help you."

Harold gave one last attack on Mia, swaying all his weight out of Billy's grip, nearly crashing to the ground. "You won't get away with it. I'll sue!"

The wiry ex-Marine quickly recovered his charge, nodding to Mia, "This way, sir." There was no way Harold would escape that iron grip a second time.

By the time she got to her cottage, the light was softening into dusk. She walked in the newly painted green door and smiled at the living room inside. It was a lovely room, comfortable and intimate. She could imagine it being the perfect honeymoon suite with its private location at the edge of the main hotel grounds. The walls were a soft white, with hints of old world moulding around the edges. The sofa looked classically formal, with faint roses in the smooth floral patterned fabric, but was incredibly comfortable. The room could have existed a hundred years ago, in the Sea Islands heyday, but had all the comforts of a modern, luxurious home.

A huge bouquet of roses almost covered the coffee table. So sweet of Maria to remember her. Always red roses for her - her husband had been a classic romantic. She sunk her nose into them and breathed in the smell. Lovely. She sat down and crossed her legs, checking the magazines laid out in an artistic fan. A perfect selection for a rainy afternoon. This was going to be a relaxing stay, Mia thought.

Tonight, she wore an elegantly cut silk floral dress and some coordinating blue spinel earrings. She added a large blue spinel ring with encircling diamonds to her ring finger and smiled at the sparkle.

Mia still wore her wedding ring, even two years after her husband's death, because it always made her think of their wedding. Leo had put the simple diamond eternity ring on her finger and winked at her. She'd almost burst out laughing in the middle of the ceremony, his comical grin was so infectious. She had a lovely engagement ring she wore frequently, of course, but she liked to mix up the jewelry she wore. It all had so many wonderful memories.

She walked through the damp night air to the hotel. It had turned a little cold tonight and she shivered in her silk dress. "Cat walking over my grave," she said to herself, smiling at the phrase.

Inside the hotel felt cozy and warm and she greeted the concierge with pleasure, "Sullivan! It's so good to see you."

The dark young man smiled back at her, "Ms. Mia! It's good to see you too. Have you had a nice day?"

"It's been a good day, up to that poor man breaking his ankle."

"Oh yes, you were the one who called it in, weren't you?" He winked wickedly at her, "Mrs. Winley already has a substitute." He grinned.

"Really? That's fast work."

"She came in and was complaining about having to dine all alone. Trey offered to prevent the catastrophe."

"Ah, Trey," Mia said thoughtfully and frowned.

"Yes, just like Trey," Sullivan smiled disdainfully. "If he doesn't marry rich, it won't be from lack of trying."

"Hannah Winley is still quite married, from what I understand."

"She won't be long if she keeps up what she's been up to," Sullivan rejoined. "I doubt she'll be rich either. There must be a prenup."

"I wish people would just come here and have fun," Mia said with sorrow.

"No worries there," the concierge rejoined, his narrow shoulders shaking with suppressed laughter. "She's having plenty of fun."

He looked around for onlookers and leaned toward her, "I'm glad I saw you today. I've a little problem I've been meaning to talk to Maria about, but I'd really prefer you handle it." He looked worried.

"Yes? What's wrong?"

"It's about Misty, the spa receptionist. You know Misty?"

"Of course. What's wrong?"

"Well, she's a sweet girl, and she's having a little trouble with Trey Sulley. He keeps showing up at her apartment at odd hours. She didn't want to go to Maria, because it would be her word against his, and she loves her job. She's going to school part time for physical therapy, and you know how we work with school hours."

"Yes, I know." Mia was concerned. "He's showing up at her apartment at night?"

"Yes, or very early, from your point of view. She lives on the island. It's just odd, and it's making her nervous." Sullivan was obviously protective of the young girl. "I don't think she's the only one whose door he shows up at, either."

"I see," Mia said thoughtfully. "I'll speak with Maria about him."

Sullivan looked more worried. "She really likes her job."

"Don't worry, I'll make sure there's no backlash on her and she's protected." Mia smiled at him, "Trust me, Maria's dealt with this kind of thing before."

Sullivan looked unconvinced. "Trey is a very smooth talker."

Mia told him firmly, "I'll handle it." She changed the subject. "So what's new and good at the Hammock Dining Room?"

"I'd try the new she crab soup. It's absolutely marvelous."

"Sounds perfect," Mia headed for the dining room. She was ushered to a quiet corner table with a good view of the restaurant. Potted palms dotted the room, giving it a tropical feel.

Her waitress, Dorrie, poured her water. "What can I bring you tonight?"

"Hi, Dorrie. I was told to try the she crab soup," Mia said. "And I feel like something hearty," Mia said. "Maybe chef's famous seafood lasagna? With perhaps a crisp Soave wine to drink?"

The waitress whisked her menu away and chattily said, "I heard you rescued Hannah Winley's companion."

"I just called the ambulance," Mia explained. "And she's already found a new escort," she nodded toward Trey Sulley and Hannah having an intimate dinner in the corner next to the piano. He leaned toward her, whispering something. Hannah shook her head and instinctively leaned back, but didn't leave the table.

"She doesn't seem to like him that much," Dorrie commented. "I'll be right back with your order, Ms. Mia."

As she watched, Hannah smiled seductively at Trey, leaned forward and whispered something. She was dripping in diamonds and sparkling with sequins, like last night. Quite a lot of brilliance for the more casual dining room. But Dorrie was right, she didn't look happy with her dinner date, despite her showgirl smile.

She looked around the long low room and saw Rebecca and Sam with eyes only for each other, a beautiful sight indeed. Trying not to catch their eyes, she left them alone in their world.

A few of the wedding guests were scattered around the room, old and new friends relaxing together now that the main event was over. Soft laughter and smiling voices mingled with the appetizing smells.

The writer, Harold Stone, sat over in a corner nursing a Scotch. He shoveled steak into his mouth, not pausing between bites. Mia didn't see how he could be tasting his food at all. After that confrontation earlier, she didn't see how he was vertical. Unfortunately, she couldn't lock unruly guests in their rooms. They were stuck with the drunk until he got unruly enough to kick out of the hotel, which was the last thing she wanted to do to such a well known writer.

His wispy assistant sat ramrod straight, as far away as she could get from him and still sit at the same table, clearly disgusted by his lack of table manners.

Mia noticed Billy and his wife, Jolie, over on the side of the dining room and gave them a friendly nod. He

nodded back, keeping one eye on Harold Stone and one
on his lovely wife. Jolie seemed happy to have a night off
from cooking for her brood of grandchildren. Mia could
hear her hearty laugh across the room, and it made her
smile. She made a mental note to send them champagne
when she ordered.

Sissy Collinsworth looked down at her menu,
actively avoiding Mia's eye. She was still in her sandy
long skirt she'd worn all day.

Mia had a lovely dinner, enjoying her seafood
lasagna comfort food. She skipped dessert tonight and
rose to go at the same time as several other people in the
restaurant.

Mia let the others weave through the room before
her. She noticed Trey stoop and hand a paper to Sam.
Odd, Mia thought. She hadn't seen Sam drop anything.
Sam glanced at it casually, then stiffened, seeming not to
notice Rebecca for the first time tonight. Trey and
Hannah brushed by her. Hannah, after a close knit
whispering laugh with Trey, continued on to her cottage.

Trey paused to talk with the concierge in the lobby,
laughing hard at something Sullivan apparently didn't
find funny at all. He noticed Mia, "Ah, Mia. I'm so glad
to see you. I wanted to apologize to you for your terrible
experience at breakfast. I took care of the problem, and
he won't be working here anymore," he smiled an
insincere grin at her.

Mia gaped at him. "Excuse me?"

"I've fired that chef Francisco González. He served
you a terrible breakfast and wasn't up to the job of

running a kitchen," he shook his head in mock despair. "He just wasn't up to the job."

"I see," Mia said icily. Personal dislike had not been a reason enough for her to fire Trey Sulley, but this might be. Of course, it was Maria's job to supervise her team. "You didn't think Maria, as the manager, should make that decision?"

"Word is she won't be manager much longer," Trey said smoothly. "She's a bit past it, isn't she? Time for some new ideas and new blood here. Get some more exciting guests than old fogies, liven this place up." he laughed heartily, not bothering to hide his disdain of several elderly guests passing him slowly. From their expressions, they weren't all that hard of hearing.

"I see," Mia repeated expressionlessly. She needed to get this scene away from the guests quickly, but she didn't want to be alone with Trey Sulley. "Sullivan, can you and Trey come to the office for a minute?"

She saw Billy kiss his wife, then wander casually in their direction as they headed for the office. Sullivan efficiently motioned one of his underlings to take charge of his desk and followed them back to Maria's office. Maria looked up as they entered, still working this late at night.

"Mia?" She looked at the little group. "What's going on? Is something wrong?" Maria purposely avoided Trey's gaze, ignoring him.

"Did you fire Francisco González?" Mia asked. She'd get her facts straight first.

"No, of course not," Maria said with confusion, smoothing her styled brown hair distractedly. "He's one of our best young chefs, training up well. I see him being head chef in a few years."

"Head chef," Trey sneered. "He can't even cook breakfast. I fired him."

"What? He hasn't been on breakfast yet," Maria said, bewildered. "He's not scheduled to train for that for another month."

Mia clarified, "I believe Mr. Sulley put him in charge of breakfast this morning."

"You what?" Maria stood up, face horrified.

"He's a chef, isn't he? Chef called in sick so I put González on," Trey said confidently. "He couldn't do the job so I fired him," he looked at Mia for the expected vote of approval.

Mia avoided his gaze and sat down with composure in a side chair. Sullivan stood behind her, his elegant lean frame ready for action.

Billy appeared in the doorway, his relaxed body standing on the balls of his feet. He turned his wrinkled face cheerfully from one speaker to the next, clearly enjoying the show. Mia glanced at him and he winked cheekily.

"You put him on breakfast with no training?" Maria was aghast. "Then fired him? May I ask why?" she said with clipped syllables.

"He had the gall to serve Mia here a lousy omelette. I heard she had to go and show him how to make one. So I fired him." Trey was proud of his prompt action.

Mia added in her own icy tones, "He had not been trained in our method. I stayed in the kitchen afterwards, and he was doing an excellent job, under the circumstances."

Maria looked at her for guidance and Mia nodded. She'd stand by Maria's decision.

"You threw him in the deep end and fired him when he wasn't perfect," Maria summed up with a frown, tapping her pencil on the desk.

She looked up with decision. "I'm afraid you're not what I'm looking for in my assistant managers, Mr. Sulley. You're fired."

"Wait a minute," Trey backpedaled briskly. "You can't fire me."

Maria repeated, "You're fired."

Trey cut in, "You can't fire me. I'll tell everything I know about you. I mean everything," he threatened vindictively.

Mia felt Billy and Sullivan shift position slightly, ready for action.

Maria continued inexorably, "You're fired, effective immediately. You have two weeks to vacate your house on the island, according to your contract. During this time, you do not have use of the facilities." She held out her hand, "Please hand me your master key card."

Trey looked to Mia for help. "Mia, don't let her do this. I thought we were getting to be friends. I was just trying to help you out. I could tell you all kinds of things about Maria here," he offered with a sly smile.

Mia stiffened, back straight as a board. "This is far from the only issue I have with you, Mr. Sulley. I had several I planned to discuss with Mrs. Sotos tomorrow. We have ample cause for your dismissal."

He protested with a sneer, "You don't run this hotel. You're not the manager here anymore. You're just a rich man's leftovers. Like you care as long as the money rolls in, and you get your fancy vacations."

Mia smiled like a crocodile, "I have the right to fire anyone I want. You're a disgrace to the hotel, and you are fired."

He made a quick move toward her and Sullivan stepped a little forward, balancing on his toes.

"Fine," he backed down and fumbled for his key card. "It's a lousy job anyway."

"I'm glad you feel that way, Mr. Sulley."

Sullivan followed him out the door, herding him like a sheepdog. Billy nodded to Mia, walking alongside their charge. He winked at them as he gently closed the door.

"Whew," Maria said.

"Yes, he's a nasty bit of work," Mia said. "I was going to recommend you let him go when we chatted tomorrow. We just needed to make sure we had documented cause. He's the type that would sue unless we have ammunition. Did you know he's been showing up at the girls' apartments at night?"

Maria said stiffly, "No, I did not know that or his ass would have been out of here long ago." She sighed, collapsing into her chair. "I clearly need to have a team meeting. I should have spotted this."

"Yes, they need to come to you with small problems before they become big ones," Mia said emphatically.

Maria toyed with a pencil. "I thought they did. Everything seemed to be going smoothly."

"It always does, until you hit a bump," Mia told her. She paused, then went on, "Are you going to tell me what he was threatening you with?"

Maria looked uncomfortably away. "Oh, Mia, it's just so embarrassing, I don't want to talk about it. Things I thought were buried so long ago." She looked down at her paperwork. "I maybe gave him one more chance than I should have to avoid the gossip but that's all. There's no way I wouldn't have fired him after he fired Francisco for no cause." She fiddled with her paperwork, "Can we talk about it tomorrow?"

"It's okay," Mia trusted her old friend and didn't want to add to her discomfort right now. "Just clean up the mess and move on." She'd find out what was going on whether Maria told her or not.

"Right," Maria said with decision. "First thing is a call to Francisco." She picked up the phone, tapping a pencil and Mia left her to it.

Rebecca stood on the balcony in her silk robe, shivering. She looked out at the dark, the lights blurring with her tears. They'd had a wonderful day. It really had been like a second honeymoon, Sam sailing and acting like when they'd met again. They'd had a wonderful dinner and then suddenly, Sam had been distant again.

He'd barely spoken when they came up, seeming angry. He hadn't even noticed the new glamorous nightgown she'd bought for a special night on their trip. He hadn't even looked at her. He'd simply put on his ratty old pajamas and pretended to go to sleep. She knew he wasn't really asleep since he wasn't snoring. He was just laying there, pretending, so he didn't have to talk to her.

There was no point in a fight. Rebecca had left for the living room of their suite, which had a sofa bed. She'd pulled it out and laid down, but she just couldn't sleep.

She heard Sam's door to the hallway close softly, muffled by the wall but still audible. He had gone out somewhere by himself, without her.

She drew the dark red robe tightly around her and swallowed the sleeping pill her doctor had given her for nights she couldn't sleep. It would take effect in a few minutes, and she wouldn't lay awake all night worrying.

She sat looking down the hotel terrace, mind starting to calm, knowing she would sleep soon. People came and went, happy voices chattering and calling. She knew what Mia meant about hotels being fun places. She loved the joy people had on vacations.

They had had so much fun today, sailing in the bay. Life had seemed simple and perfect. And now it was back to this, Sam hiding from her, and her hiding from him. Where had he gone in the middle of the night?

No, she wouldn't think about that tonight. She'd let the medicine lull her to sleep. Any decisions she made tomorrow would be made with a clear head.

The air was heavy and still with hardly any wind. Oppressive. She looked at the scattering of people walking through the palm tree shadows. The palmetto fronds made a clackety noise, percussion to the soft splash of waves. Glasses clinked and guests talked in cheerful voices. She spotted Mia leaving by the back way and strolling down the beach a little, then returning to her cottage.

That sweet young chef who made the wonderful pastries came out carrying a bag, walking very fast down the beach toward the apartments. Late for him to be at work, she thought vaguely.

Maria, the manager, came past, also walking down the beach, her flashlight disappearing in the distance. She looked upset, her steps rapid and clipped. Rebecca thought she wasn't the only one having a bad night.

That assistant manager, Trey, hurried after Maria. He walked angrily down the beach in great strides. She saw his flashlight disappear through the palmetto palms.

She saw Sam appear on the beach, dressed in the same clothes he'd worn today and walking down to the sand. Her heart cried out. She didn't understand what was happening to them. He disappeared past the palmettos, walking through the wave washed sand.

A wedding party went down to the beach, chattering with great bursts of laughter. The men seemed happily tipsy and their wives not much different. They walked through the splashing waves, pants rolled up and sand between their toes. It was good to see people having fun.

Beyond the warm lights, the inky black of the ocean reached out forever under the domed dark sky. Palm trees clattered in the ocean breeze, and the sounds of revelers gradually faded as the night claimed them.

She tried to stay awake to hear Sam come in, but the medicine lulled her to sleep. Eventually, she found her way back to her solitary bed. She hadn't seen Sam again.

3

The Morning After

Dorrie found the body in the morning, walking to work from her apartment. Trey Sulley lay at the edge of the surf, face up with his legs moving in the water. His brown hair was slicked back from his face and covered in wet sand. His eyes stared into nothing, and blood covered his chest.

Dorrie stood there a moment, frozen and staring. The ocean washed the shore, back and forth, and Trey's legs moved with the water, back and forth, like some dance of the dead. Nothing else moved. A seagull shrieked, releasing her from her trance.

She screamed, running to the hotel, the seagulls came with her, screeching, and the sand held her feet as she ran. She made it inside the hospitality team quarters, still screaming.

"Dorrie?" Sullivan ran to her, his elegant shirt firmly tucked and every hair still in place. "Calm down, don't disturb the guests. What's going on?"

"Trey's dead!"

"What?"

"He's on the beach, dead." She shivered, "I think he's been stabbed. There's blood everywhere." She started shaking uncontrollably and Sullivan wrapped a towel around her.

"Shouldn't we call the police?" Dorrie said after a minute. She was getting her breath back.

He stared at her. "Yes, yes, of course." He went to the hotel phone and called the police. When he hung up with the police, he called Maria. When she understood what had happened, she ordered him to the beach to keep early rising guests away from the body. She was calling groundskeepers to block off the area, but they would take a few minutes to arrive. He could hear her rapidly dressing as she barked orders at him.

Sullivan hung up and looked at Dorrie, not wanting to leave her alone. "Are you okay?"

"Yeah," she told him dully.

"I have to go prevent someone else from getting a nasty shock like you."

She looked up, her face still green, "Yeah, the others will be coming from the houses. You'd better go." He poured her a hot coffee with tons of sugar.

"You drink this. Sugar's good for shock, right?" he smiled reassuringly at her. "I'll be back as soon as I can."

She nodded and he left, running.

Sullivan stopped a little way from the body, where he could see guests coming from the hotel and the crew coming from housing. He looked at Trey's body as little as possible. He felt sweat pouring down his face, even in the cool morning air. He ran a hand through his hair then smoothed it down. The police would be here soon, thank God. He kept glancing at Trey's body and forcing himself not to look, not to remember this in his nightmares.

He saw two team members, maybe Misty and Harrison, walking towards him and the body. The body, not Trey anymore. No guests the other way. He signaled them to take the inland path and they did, looking behind them with curiosity. He was glad they couldn't see much from that distance. He didn't think he'd forget Trey's staring eyes and the blood for a very long time.

When Sullivan saw the police uniforms in the distance, he ran toward them, surrendering his post with relief. He gave his name then returned thankfully to the hotel, collapsing beside Dorrie in the hospitality team room.

"Well, that was fun," he said sardonically. "The police are here."

Several of the crew milled around, pushing more sweet coffee at Dorrie. No one seemed to know what do next or want to leave the hospitality team room. They felt safer in a clump.

Maria walked in and gave Dorrie a hug. "You poor thing. Are you okay?"

Dorrie smiled, her face starting to resume its normal color. "I'll be fine in a few minutes."

"If you think you're okay to work, have breakfast and then go ahead. If you need time off, take it."

"I'll be fine," Dorrie grimaced. "I really couldn't eat."

"Okay, take a meal break when you feel like you can. Don't go too long with an empty stomach." She turned to the rest of the room. "Let's get this show on the road," Maria pointed to each in turn, giving them their duties for the morning. People's faces relaxed with concrete tasks to accomplish in the crisis. "This is a terrible thing to happen to one of our own."

"I thought he was fired," Sullivan muttered.

"It's a terrible thing," Maria repeated over him. "But we need the hotel running as smoothly as ever and for guests to not notice one thing wrong. I've got the landscape team blocking off the beach around the police. They'll take care of hiding the incident," she stumbled a little, "from our guests. The guests will find out, of course, but let's try to wait until we have more to tell them."

"What about Ms. Mia?" Dorrie questioned.

"Oh, Mia." Maria pursed her mouth like she'd sucked a lemon. "I'll call her now. Better she finds out from me than on her morning walk. Thanks, Dorrie."

"What if the police want to talk with us?" Sullivan asked.

"Cooperate with the police as much as possible. If they need to question you, talk to your superior and get someone to cover for you. Then just answer every question that they have. If you have any help to offer the police, give it."

She looked them over, her troops, kind brown eyes considering each in turn. "I know the gossip will get around like it always does. I fired Trey last night because he was a disruptive influence. Someone did stab him, and I hope to God it wasn't one of you. I know it wasn't me." She smiled grimly. "If you feel like you need a lawyer, especially if you're innocent and have anything could be misconstrued, talk to me right now. I can help you organize some legal guidance." Maria looked at the shocked, unhappy faces around her and looked down at her hands. "This is a terrible thing to happen to our hotel."

She stood up with decision. "Okay, let's get going. We don't want anyone's vacation disturbed by this."

While the team quietly assembled, she held Sullivan back, "We'll need to tell them about last night and firing him. When I talk to the police, I'll tell them to contact you and Mia. Just pull in one of the receptionists to cover for you."

He nodded and left.

She went to her office. It was usually such a happy place with warm white walls and bookcases housing reference books and her treasures, a few shells and mementos, but mostly photos of her loved ones. Maria smiled at a photo of her much younger self and Mia at Mia's wedding. They lifted champagne flutes and lights sparkled all around them. It seemed so long ago and them so young. She picked up the phone.

As soon as she got Maria's call, Mia dressed quicker than she had in years. She wore subdued colors of rust and tan, the quietest in her wardrobe here. She texted her stepson, Mark, the company CEO, with the bare facts. Promising to keep him up to date with details, she hurried to the main building. Sullivan greeted her with a quiet unhappy nod, "Maria's in her office."

Mia ran to Maria and gave her a hug, "Oh, honey, this is just terrible."

Maria hugged her back. "I know. And I fired him last night too." She put her face in her hands, "It's just awful."

Mia patted her on the back. "It is. I didn't like him, but he was so young. It's always terrible when people don't get a chance to," she trailed off.

"Well, our priority is the hotel. We can do something about that. The police will solve his murder."

"There's no way guests won't find out," Maria said despondently.

"We just need to step up. You're right, there is no way guests won't hear about this, and we don't want a mass exodus."

"What can we possibly do?"

"Let's make their stay just a little nicer," Mia suggested. "Maybe complimentary spa or golf passes? All the extras that if the guests leave, no one is using anyway. So some freebies, we lose a little profit, but most people will stay here despite a little unpleasantness." She thought a minute, "What have the police said?"

"They were very nice under the circumstances and said they'd try to keep as out of the way as possible. The hotel is a major part of the county's economy, after all. They want to keep things quiet."

Mia nodded.

"They'll control access on and off the island at the bridge, so we don't need to worry about press yet. They need to speak with any guests or hospitality team that had direct contact with Trey, especially in the last day or two. I've already instructed the team to talk to them." She shook her head. "I also said I'd organize a lawyer if they felt they needed one, especially if they were innocent."

"Good. Anything our resort team does here reflects on the hotel," Mia agreed. "I don't want any innocent employees wrongly accused and dragged through the press." She frowned, "Frankly, I want to know exactly what happened. Trey was a harassment case waiting to happen, if I'm any judge."

"Yes, I know," Maria said dismally. "He came so highly recommended, absolutely glowing references. He was last at the St. Johns in San Francisco as an assistant manager and said he wanted to move to a warmer climate. He seemed nice and reasonably efficient." She sighed, "I think he went off his best behavior about a month ago. I'd spoken to him a few times about it, but he didn't seem to care."

She looked away, embarrassed, "He'd dug up some past history I didn't want gossiped about. I probably gave him one too many warnings instead of just dismissing him."

Maria held up her hands in frustration. "I also needed definite cause to fire him. I couldn't fire him because I didn't like him, and he just wasn't a good fit for the hotel. I didn't want a wrongful dismissal suit against the hotel. If I'd known he was harassing the girls, it would have been cause for dismissal, and I'd have fired him that day. I was hoping he'd just crawl away and out of my hotel."

Mia said thoughtfully, "So he snooped." She looked at Maria, "I'm guessing your secret wasn't common knowledge."

"No," Maria's tone was clipped.

"Then he must have snooped. Did you pay blackmail?" She posed the question matter of factly. She was going to know the worst of it, so she could protect her friend.

"Of course not," Maria said, aghast. "I'd never do that."

"But someone else might have," Mia said thoughtfully. "A hotel would be a perfect environment for a blackmailer. There are lots of secrets here."

4

What You Can Tell About a Person

There was a discreet knock at the door and it opened. "Captain Daniels to see you, ma'am."

Maria stood and warmly shook hands with the policeman, smartly attired in a crisp blue uniform and standing to attention. "I'm glad you're here to guide us through this terrible time, Tom. Do you remember Mrs. Mia Spinel?"

"I remember Danny," Mia said enthusiastically. "Let's see, I think you were a lifeguard one summer and also, was it landscaping?" She smiled at him as a long lost friend.

"It's been a long time since anyone called me Danny, Mrs. Spinel." He shook hands with Mia, and she gestured to a chair.

"Please, Danny, do call me Mia," she told him. "That's a long time ago, and you're a police captain now. Time flies."

"Yes, ma'am. Mia," he quickly corrected himself. He sat very straight in his comfortable chair, with military posture. "Well, Mr. Sulley was definitely murdered. He was stabbed in the heart with a thin knife." He shook his head sadly. "It's a sad day when one human could do that to another."

Maria suggested, "There were a few things I wanted to speak about with you, Tom. We had some problems with Mr. Sulley that culminated in him being fired last night."

Captain Daniels leaned forward at attention. "What kind of problems?"

"One was him showing up in at least one girl's apartment at night. You remember we have a semi dorm situation with little efficiencies for younger team members?"

"I spent a summer or two there myself," he smiled in remembrance.

"That's right," Mia agreed. "Our spa receptionist, Misty, had problems with him. From what I understand, some of the others may have as well."

"Interesting," he mused. "So maybe it was self defense?" He shook his head, "That would have been a sharp knife to carry around, and the beach isn't an apartment."

"Most of the resort crew walks along the beach to their apartments at night rather than the main road," Maria broke in. "I usually do myself. It's a nice wind down after a long day. And there're less bugs in the ocean breeze."

Captain Daniels pulled out his notebook. "Let me get these times down. What time did you fire Mr. Sulley?"

He wrote all the pertinent facts down in a neat schedule, Mia noticed as she unashamedly looked around his shoulder.

"I've reserved the conference room in the Heron Building for the police," Maria said efficiently. "I thought a little privacy and room to work would be best for you... and for our guests," she said ruefully.

"Perfect," he said crisply, standing at attention. "I'll try to keep as discrete as possible, but we will have find the culprit."

"Of course," Maria agreed. "I hope you find him as soon as possible."

"Could you please send," he looked down at his notes, "Misty and Sullivan there in fifteen minutes?"

"Of course. I've instructed all team members who interacted with Mr. Sulley yesterday or have information for you to see you today. I want this terrible thing solved." Maria smiled, "Would coffee and doughnuts speed the process?"

"Keep the coffee coming, please," he said appreciatively. "I'll need to talk to you both again soon, but I'll just get an overview, watch the security footage. I will probably need to search some rooms as well."

Mia put her hand confidingly on his arm. She had to crane her neck up to look him directly in his dark brown eyes. "Could I please be there while you're questioning my team, Danny?"

He shook his head decisively no. "Not possible."

"I'm concerned, especially about the younger team members. They're under my care, my responsibility."

He smiled down at her, "I understand, but I just can't do it, Mia."

She stepped back, disappointed but resigned.

"I'll tell you what, I'll let you, as the hotel representative, be present when we go through the staff or guest rooms, except Mr. Sulley's. That should salve your conscience." He looked back at her as he stepped out the door, "And satisfy your curiosity." Danny grinned as he closed the door softly.

Danny whistled as he went out of the main hotel toward the Heron Building. It wasn't the first time he'd been back here since he'd worked here, by any means. He usually took his wife to dinner here on their anniversary. She liked to dress up and eat a fancy meal and they could afford it, now. So why not if it made her happy?

It wasn't his kind of thing, but it sure was nice to know they'd be fed well during the investigation. Maria would see to that. It made a change from drug dealer's dens and sordid crimes in back alleys. Though murder was a terrible thing, wherever it happened.

He always responded to Spinel Hotel calls himself if he was working. It was nice to see the place again, stay familiar with it. Plus the resort was a major source of revenue for the county and that mattered too. Good for the police chief to stay on good terms with the hotel.

Mia would definitely butt into his investigation. He'd never known her not to be involved in everything. The stories of her interference were legend. But she wouldn't try to get him to ignore a rich suspect, simply because they were rich. She'd always been fair to him when he worked there, even when he was a lowly lifeguard.

He remembered back when she'd been manager at the hotel. A rich blonde divorcee complained about Danny sexually harassing her. When he was a teenage boy, he'd never even have dreamt of looking at a middle aged female guest, but he sure had been up to something in the woman's overactive imagination. Mia had his back then, quietly reassigning him to other parts of the hotel while the crazy woman was a guest. She'd made sure no other young male staff interacted with his accuser either.

He knew now that accusation, if it had been recorded officially, could have ruined his future career. That long ago false accusation could even have kept him from his dream job of police chief. Now he was older, he realized to most employers, the rich customer was always right. He thanked his lucky stars Mia had tactfully kept the incident from becoming public.

Danny wouldn't exactly say he owed her, but he'd sure as hell say he respected her and her judgment.

Unfortunately, he also realized every move he made on the hotel grounds was going to be supervised and second guessed by Mia. He wasn't much looking forward to that.

With a heavy sigh, he started planning his investigation.

After Mia left, Maria put her head down on her hands for a minute. Everything was falling apart at once. Life had been perfect. A happy marriage, kids doing well, her dream job where she got to live on this gorgeous island.

And in one moment, it had all crashed to the ground like a house of cards.

Maria massaged her temples and tried very hard to think of what to do next.

Trey had blackmailed her; she admitted it to herself, if never completely to anyone else. He hadn't asked for money, but he'd been able to get away with all sorts of things she'd never have allowed in another assistant manager. She'd bided her time, collecting incidents so she could fire him without his gossip becoming public.

But last night had been the final straw. What was past was past, anyhow. She'd have fired his ass whether Mia had been there or not. She still didn't know whether she was glad Mia had witnessed it or just plain mortified.

She'd walked down the beach last night, thinking about the long talk Mia would insist on in the morning. Mia didn't ever let things just go—she was like a honey badger. You might think she was letting you decide for yourself, but that was just a temporary misconception.

No, she didn't need to see the future in the stars to know Mia would be talking to her in the morning.

Last night, she had walked right past where Trey was murdered. She wondered if he'd been running to catch up with her or just walking home. The beach she walked every day contained a murderer. She shivered, looking at the silver framed photo of her family on her desk, praying for strength and guidance, a return to her perfect life.

No matter, past was past and things didn't get undone. She straightened up in her comfortable office chair. It was time to start planning how to get out of the mess Trey and his murderer had caused.

Mia would take care of the murderer. Maria's job was the hotel.

At breakfast, Mia looked at her team closely, but she didn't see any trace of anything off. Just the expected shock at having someone die in their midst. No obvious signs of guilt she could find.

Dorrie served coffee and her omelet with professional cheer. Her eyes were red from crying, but makeup made most of the evidence unobtrusive.

After breakfast, Mia wandered over to the spa building where Misty worked, thinking the girl would be done with the police, and Mia could ask her a few questions.

Misty was there at her organically curved desk beside a serene koi pond and waterfall. "Hi, Ms. Mia, ready for the spa?" She efficiently pulled her appointment book up on her computer.

"Not quite yet, Misty. I really came to check on you," she looked sympathetically at the girl. Misty's smooth round cheeks weren't curved in a smile, which was completely foreign to her normal demeanor.

"I'm really fine, Ms. Mia."

"Did the police treat you alright?" She couldn't imagine Danny doing anything poorly. She'd never seen a lifeguard with so much attention on the job he was doing, rather than the pretty girls in bikinis trying their best to distract him.

"They were fine. I saw Captain Daniels. He said he'd worked here as a kid?" Mia nodded agreement. "He was nice, just asked me questions about Trey showing up at my apartment and stuff."

"So what exactly happened, Misty?"

"He'd just show up real late, about two am and bang on my door. I opened it the first time since I thought something was wrong. I had to shove him to get him out of my apartment." Misty was obviously uncomfortable.

"Why didn't you go to Mrs. Sotos?"

"Well, I like my job, and you know, I thought he was just drunk. I just didn't open it after that first time and kept the chain on." She shook her head and fiddled with her smooth brown hair. "It was creepy, but I think he did it to all the girls."

Mia sat back, horrified. "Honey, that's exactly the sort of thing you need to tell Mrs. Sotos about. That shouldn't happen here."

"Yeah, well," Misty's blue eyes darted around the room, "I think she had her own problems with him. I heard them arguing a few times."

"I see," Mia was going to have a very serious discussion with Maria soon. "If anything, and I repeat, anything like this or anything else that makes you uncomfortable happens at the hotel, you need to tell Mrs. Sotos immediately." She explained, "Mrs. Sotos was trying to find cause to fire Mr. Sulley. Last night, when she heard about your problems and him firing Francisco with no authorization, that did it." She didn't mention Maria hadn't heard about Misty until afterwards.

She stood up, "If you know of anyone else who had problems, tell them to go to the police. They need to know everything."

Misty looked scared and worried, "Yes, ma'am."

"We want to solve this murder as soon as possible so we can go back to normal," Mia gave her a reassuring smile.

Captain Daniels was striding with a policewoman toward the main hotel. From the look on his face, he'd hoped to avoid catching Mia's eyes, but gracefully gave way. "We've reviewed the security footage, ma'am, and we have a few people we want to question further and whose rooms we want to search."

He gestured to his companion. She had short brown hair under a uniform cap, a neat evidence collection bag and bright blue eyes that missed nothing. "Sergeant

Jessica Waters, this is Mia Spinel, one of the hotel owners. She's going to observe while we examine the rooms."

"Ma'am," she acknowledged firmly.

"It's nice to meet you, Sergeant Waters," Mia paused. "Now, have I met you before?" she asked. "You seem very familiar."

"Olympic rowing, ma'am," a flash of pride showed. "We brought home the gold."

"That's it!" Mia said. "Congratulations. I know you're an asset to," she looked at his pleading face, "Captain Daniels and the police investigation here." She smiled benignly and followed their erect figures to the main hotel.

The police opened Maria's office door and she looked up with a worried greeting, "What can I do for you?"

"Mrs. Sotos," he put a printed screenshot down on her desk. "When I reviewed the security footage, I noticed Mr. Sulley leaving very shortly after you left the hotel and walking in the same direction."

"Oh," Maria looked at the photo. "Oh, yes. I see." She thought a moment. "I don't think I saw him at all. My house lies a little past the turnoff to the others, and I was thinking so I wasn't paying much attention." She smiled grimly, "I doubt he would have passed me without a word after his dismissal, and I don't remember anyone at all passing me."

"May we search your house?"

"For what?"

"Evidence connecting you with Mr. Sulley or his murder. A stabbing involves blood and a knife. Also anything else that would connect you to the crime. We will be doing the same to all potential suspects. The sooner we do it, the more chance we have of finding bloodstains."

"Oh. Oh, yes," Maria repeated dully. "I think, Captain Daniels," she said formally, "I need to tell you something." She drew a deep breath, glanced at Mia, and continued, "I did not kill Mr. Sulley. However, Mr. Sulley was," she hesitated again, "blackmailing is too strong a word, harassing, taunting? Something along those lines at any rate."

She sighed and Captain Daniels got out his notebook. "I've been married a long time. Javier and I met when we were kids." She tapped a pencil on her notebook, then forced herself to continue. "Javier was so stupid and so young," she smiled ruefully, looking back. "He went out drinking one night. One of the guys decided to rob a gas station while Javier was waiting in the car because the clerk wouldn't sell him beer. Idiot."

She looked down at the pencil, rolling it between her fingers. "Javier was sixteen and they charged him with driving the getaway car. He didn't even know about it until the cops pulled them over." She cleared her throat roughly. "He went to jail," tears welled in her eyes. "He helped the prosecutor. Finally they believed him and set him free with a clean record. He's a good man," she said. "One mistake didn't ruin our lives. We've worked so hard to be where we are." She looked at Mia, "One night, one stupid mistake."

Mia nodded with silent understanding.

"He was blackmailing you?" Captain Daniels went on.

"I'd never pay blackmail," Maria held up her hands. "I mean, it's public record. Javier, he's an accountant, might have some problems with a few clients, but on the whole it would just be terribly embarrassing to us both."

She went on, "I have a policy of two strikes and you're out with the hotel. I didn't fire Mr. Sulley after he'd made several mistakes. I probably should have, but I try to give employees a fair chance to improve, and he'd come with excellent references, from the St. Johns in San Francisco, no less. He acted like he had scored off me, let me know he knew about my husband's past conviction and became steadily more disrespectful. His completely circumventing me and firing Francisco was the last straw. And then I heard about him harassing the girls. I can't believe I waited so long to fire him."

She was clearly more concerned about Mia's opinion than Captain Daniels'.

He said, "Well, that makes sense. I wish you hadn't picked that time to go home—it puts you where you have motive and opportunity." He held up his hands in self defense. "I agree it's not much of a motive." He smiled grimly, "I have a few more photos for you to identify if you can," and fanned them out on her desk.

Mia came over to look. The elderly birdwatching couple she'd noticed were photographed hand in hand walking through the sand. His pants were neatly rolled to his knees and she was carrying her shoes.

"That's the Brownings. I can't imagine them murdering anyone," Maria sighed. "The problem is I can't imagine anyone murdering Trey. He was like a mosquito, annoying. Always buzzing around."

"Mosquitos kill more humans than any other animal," Captain Daniels stated flatly. He tapped the photo. "It appears the Brownings never came back from their walk."

"I think they're birdwatchers," Mia supplied. "I'm sure they went to look for owls or something."

"Most probably." He pointed to the next photo and Mia frowned.

"That's Sam Forrest," she volunteered. "His wife works for Spinel Hotels out of Atlanta. They're here on vacation." Sam certainly looked very angry, in what she could see of the night photo. "Oh, dear," she thought.

Sissy Collinsworth walked through the surf in the next photo, skirt in the water as usual. "She's been organizing a charity event with Mr. Sulley," Maria told him. "I think there was some friction between them, but I don't know about what."

Captain Daniels nodded, "We'll find out."

The next photo showed Harold Stone. He was carrying a bottle and wandering up the beach.

"Harold Stone, the writer," Mia identified him.

Captain Daniels wrote a note and shuffled another photo on the desk.

Francisco González showed up, carrying a small bag. The expression on his face was not happy. "That's the young chef whose firing precipitated the unpleasantness yesterday," Maria said. "I'm sure he's just carrying his personal equipment back to his house."

She turned to Mia, "I wasn't able to get hold of him yesterday evening." She tapped the photo. "I guess we know why now. Poor kid was cleaning out his locker. I called him this morning and told him," she held out her hands in confusion, "all that happened. He's planning to be back on duty this afternoon, as usual."

Sergeant Waters sharply asked, "So he didn't know about Mr. Sulley being fired and his job secure when this photo was taken?"

"Not unless he talked to one of the crew on his way home," Maria said. "I'm sure the gossip mill knew by then."

"We'll find out who he talked to and when," Captain Daniels told her. "Are there any other people Mr. Sulley had an argument or even close contact with in the past few days?"

Mia coughed discreetly, "While I was biking, I saw one of the guests leaving his house in the morning. They appeared to be on extremely good terms. Allison Jayton."

"Hmm, there's always the possibility of a lovers' quarrel. I'll need to check her out. Anyone else?"

"He had dinner last night with Hannah Winley, another of our guests." Maria told him, "Her husband is the billionaire, Arthur Winley," she warned him.

"Thanks, I'll tread carefully."

"The young man who was her, umm, companion, had an accident yesterday and went to the hospital. From what I understand, she ran into Trey in the lobby, and he volunteered to keep her company at dinner." Mia frowned, "Of course, if he had progressed to actual blackmail then he might have had something to threaten her with."

"Her companion," the police detective said thoughtfully. "Yes, that's worth thinking about."

Maria offered, "There was quite an argument a few nights ago. You remember the night you arrived, Mia?" she said, turning to her. "Harold Stone had lost his laptop with his latest book on it. He is a best selling author, you know. We were quite concerned it had been stolen because he'd had some trouble with his key card earlier. He started yelling in the lobby at Mr. Sulley, accusing him of theft. Trey went over and found his laptop tucked under his chair where he'd left it. Harold still seemed to blame Mr. Sulley. He kept yelling at Trey about stealing from him. He had to be ushered from the lobby." Maria shook her head in disgust.

"Interesting," Captain Daniels made a note. "And the problem with the key card system was just Mr. Stone's room?"

"No, it was all the guest rooms and safes in the main building, but Trey fixed it almost immediately," Maria looked startled and repeated, "Trey fixed it almost immediately. I hope ...," she trailed off.

"I see," Captain Daniels closed his notebook. "Well, that gives me some starting points. If you or your staff thinks of any other incidents involving Mr. Sulley, please let me know immediately." He looked at Mia. "Are you still joining us on room searches, Ms. Mia?"

"Of course." Mia followed him down the hall.

"Hopefully the guests will cooperate, and I won't need search warrants," he thought aloud. "I think I'll visit Mrs. Winley first, before she decides to leave. I don't want to deal with lawyers of that caliber."

"I believe she's in one of the cottages, Palmetto Bluff," Mia told him.

"That's over on the side, right? The very private one," Danny strode toward the pretty cottage on the very edge of the complex. It was isolated from the main hotel, shielded by large palmettos and azaleas. "Since she could have a team of lawyers here immediately, maybe you'd better explain why we're here."

Mia knocked briskly, "Mrs. Winley?" She knocked again, "Mrs. Winley, I need to speak with you."

"Coming," a bleary voice finally answered. "What do you want?" A disheveled blonde head peeked through the chained opening.

"Good morning, Mrs. Winley, I'm so sorry to disturb you. I'm Mia Spinel, one of the hotel owners. There's a problem the police need your help with." Hannah looked past her at the uniformed police, clearly puzzled and hungover.

Captain Daniels stepped forward and said in his most soothing voice, "Mrs. Winley, I'm sorry to bring you bad news, but your last night's dining companion, Mr. Trey Sulley, has been found murdered on the beach."

She gasped in horror and opened the door wide in shock. "Murdered? How awful!"

"I'd like to find out what you talked about last night at dinner. We want to get an idea of what he did his last day that might have led to his murder."

Hannah's mouth still hung open, but she motioned them inside with a vague hand.

What had been one of Spinel Hotels's most exclusive cottages was an absolute pigsty. Mia knew the maids cleaned at least once every day, so Hannah did a lot of damage in a single day. Clutter heaped everywhere, discarded tennis racquets, silky sarongs, expensive bags. A beautiful flower arrangement was shoved to one side of the coffee table and a selection of remote controls took their place. Two wine glasses sat on the bare wood of the table, marring the finish in a whitened puddle. She tightened her lips, looking at the devastated room.

She had to move a sweater and damp bathing suit off a chair to sit down. She uncomfortably perched on as little of the damp spot as possible. Mia never could believe what some people would do to a lovely hotel room.

Hannah Winley was talking, "I just can't believe he's dead. I had dinner with him last night."

She looked very young and ridiculous in her stained Leavers lace robe with last night's makeup smeared across her face. "We didn't talk about anything much. I mean, I knew he was like the manager, but he didn't really register, you know?" She shrugged, "I was just saying how I hate to eat alone and he offered, you know?"

"Of course, Mrs. Winley," Captain Daniels said smoothly. "Very natural. Can you tell me what you discussed at dinner?"

"Um, well, the food," she said flatly. "It was good." She dredged her mind. "I guess the hotel. Like, did I like the beach and if I'd been out on the water." She shivered with dislike. "I hate boats."

"I see," he said. "Anything else you can think of?"

"Not really," Hannah shrugged. "What else is there to talk about?" Her robe fell half off her shoulder, revealing she wore nothing underneath. She didn't seem to notice.

Mia smiled at Danny's firmly averted gaze.

"Since Mr. Sulley was stabbed, the murderer might have a knife and bloodstains still in their room. While we don't see you as a prime suspect," he smiled reassuringly at her, "We'd like to eliminate you as quickly as possible so you can go on with your vacation. May we have your permission to search your room for the knife and bloodstains?"

"Oh, oh, I don't know," she looked confused. "Maybe my husband's lawyers need to check?" She looked to them for advice.

Mia told her, "If you've done anything wrong, Mrs. Winley, of course you should call your lawyers immediately." She looked at her, "But perhaps you'd simply like to remove yourself from the suspect list as quickly as possible before anything," she looked meaningfully at Hannah, "anything at all gets in the press?"

Hannah turned white, looking very young, and nodded fervently.

"I've known Captain Daniels for a long time," Mia said. "He's agreed to let me overlook any hotel guest searches, to protect our guests' interests." She smiled at Hannah, "Why don't you go to the spa and have a little refresh while they search? It'll be on the house to compensate you for this stressful experience."

Hannah looked hesitant, fingers catching in her tangled hair. "I don't know."

"Go on, Mrs. Winley," the detective urged. "There's no point in you waiting around while we search. Please don't leave the island in case we need to ask you more questions."

She finally nodded, went into her bedroom with Sergeant Waters to get dressed, and headed for the spa.

"I wish she'd washed her face," Mia commented after she'd left. She quickly texted Maria to warn the spa Hannah was coming.

Danny simply surveyed the room, grimacing in disgust. "All the money in the world doesn't keep people from living like pigs, does it?" He sighed and began to check the mess for a knife and blood stained clothes.

Mia wandered into the bedroom and shook her head. "Such a mess." The room looked like a tornado had gone off in it. Diamonds tumbled on the vanity and thousand dollar dresses were tossed on the floor. She moved a gossamer swim wrap aside with her foot, trying to find a place to stand.

"I know. What a mess," Sergeant Waters said, coming up beside her. "Try not to touch anything, please, ma'am."

"Of course," Mia agreed graciously.

They bagged all the knives in the kitchen as a matter of course. Mia texted Maria to send replacements, not that Hannah cooked.

Mia looked at Hannah's dressing table, so unlike her own. Instead of a few carefully chosen elegant bottles, it was covered in tiny expensive bottles of cosmetics. Instead of Mia's single perfume, ornate perfume bottles covered the table. She counted at least ten eye shadow palettes, large to small. Powder dusted the whole, diamond necklaces glittered and several sets of valuable earrings lay scattered across the dusted table glass.

Mia noticed one of the many powders visible on the table that seemed to be an odd white in a little china box. "Oh no, I don't need drugs found at this hotel," she thought. "I hope they don't notice that." She was sure they would and began writing press statements, removing the hotel from any suspicion of drug trafficking, in her head.

She went out on the porch for some air. Taking a deep breath of the warm sea breeze, she looked around. She noticed the security cameras were angled in such a way Hannah's door wasn't covered, probably for privacy purposes. "Officer Daniels," she called and pointed at the cameras. "I'm not sure anyone would know if Hannah left her cottage last night." She pointed at a path winding along the coast. "She could easily have followed that path to access the beach."

He nodded, "I'm not sure she would have noticed the cameras at night, but it would be a natural direction for her to go to the beach at night."

He looked at her, "There appears to be a suspicious white powder on her makeup table."

She nodded, looking away.

"I think it's outside the scope of my search here," he told her. "We've documented it and confiscated what appears to be cocaine. We've found no bloodstains and removed several knives but nothing that looks suspicious for the murder." He sighed, "I don't need the hassle of her expensive lawyers descending on me about a drug charge when what I need is to solve a murder. I could care less about her destroying her own life as long as she's not a murderer too. Perhaps you might quietly take her aside and explain why her stash is gone? You might also tell her it would be a very bad idea for her to leave the island or try to get more drugs on it."

Mia nodded in relief. "I'll tell her. Is she still a suspect?"

He stated emphatically, "We have a potential blackmail motive with her affair, drugs found in her cottage and ample opportunity to leave her cottage with no one watching. If we can prove she actually was being blackmailed, it's a very strong motive." He looked at her with a wry grimace, "I wouldn't want to arrest a billionaire's wife without a lot more evidence, though."

"I wouldn't either. So you're done here?"

"On to the next," he said. "Let's go see your young chef."

Francisco González lived in the small resort team apartment complex near the end of the island. He came to the door, bleary eyed and obviously barely awake. When he saw the police and Mia, he was startled but quickly asked them to come in.

"Have you talked to Maria?" Mia quickly said.

"Yeah, she came by a few minutes ago. I left my phone off and just went to sleep last night," he shook his head. "I couldn't believe I'd been fired. And now someone's killed Trey. He was a jerk, but—wow, no one deserves a thing like that."

"You were seen going down the beach shortly before Mr. Sulley left," Captain Daniels said. "Did you see him or anyone else?"

"No, no one."

"He seemed to be hurrying down the beach, possibly to catch up with you."

Francisco shook his head emphatically. "I didn't see him. If I had, I might have punched him, but kill him with a knife? No way."

He looked at Mia, "I like my job. I'm glad I have it back, but kill for it? No way."

"I should hope not," Mia said primly. "I am glad you're still with us, however."

Captain Daniels coughed and continued, "You were carrying a bag when you left."

"Yeah, I went back to get my equipment since I figured I'd be leaving soon. I didn't want to face the others after being fired. I just went after the kitchen would have been cleaned and got my knives and stuff." He realized what he'd said and looked uncomfortable.

"Your knives?" Sergeant Waters repeated, aghast.

Mia quickly explained, "All chefs have their own knives that are their personal property. They're usually extremely valuable and very important to the chef."

"Yeah, but you're saying you were carrying knives right next to where someone was knifed? That's a bit of a coincidence." Sergeant Waters vibrated, on high alert.

"You want to see them?"

"Of course, Mr. González," said Captain Daniels. "We need to test them for blood."

Francisco went across the room and grabbed a neat bag. Sergeant Waters stood up, hand on her gun. Captain Daniels remained seated, patiently waiting.

Francisco placed the bag on the coffee table in front of Captain Daniels. "Please, go through what you like." He frowned, "I do cut meat so there might be blood traces, even after sanitizing. But no human blood, of course." He looked at the captain uncertainly, "You can test that, right?"

"Yes," Captain Daniels told him. "Can you please check the bag to make sure nothing is missing?" He looked at his sergeant, "Please note down what's in the bag." She nodded, warily sitting back down with her notebook.

Francisco opened it and drew out his knife roll. He unrolled the worn leather and displayed his knives, "See, none are missing." Each slot held a well cared for knife.

Captain Daniels nodded, "Seems to be all there. What else is in there?"

"Spare clothes, water bottle, all of those things." He opened the bag and showed them, pulling the ordinary items out. He closed it and pushed it toward the captain, "Please, take it, prove my innocence of this crime."

"I'd like to search your apartment as well," Captain Daniels told him. "Looking for blood stains or the weapon."

"Of course," Francisco agreed, "Search anywhere you would like. I want this over with and my innocence proven for all to see."

The police began their search of the small neat apartment. Everything was precisely in place. There was no clutter. Beside the tv, in pride of place, sat several family photos. Mia wandered over to see them.

"Your family?" There was an old photo of a dignified young man and beautiful woman on their wedding day and more recent ones of the same smiling older woman and two girls. One happy family scene showed them at Disney World, a younger Francisco sheepishly wearing mouse ears.

"Yeah, my mom and sisters live near Mérida. They're planning on visiting me later this year, after the busy season. Maybe Christmas, even."

"They look very happy," Mia said. "And that's a beautiful area. You must be missing it and them."

"I am," Francisco admitted. "But I wanted to work in top restaurants, really learn about great kitchens."

"Do you want to open your own restaurant someday?"

"I hope so. It is my dream. I'm still learning right now," He grinned. "Yesterday I learned how to make an omelette."

"There's always something new to learn about food." Mia told him, "Don't forget, Spinel Hotels likes moving promising young chefs around to different hotels. So when you're ready to move on to work under a different chef, consider going to another restaurant with us." She smiled, "That way, your vacation days really start to add up after a few years and you can have a long visit with your family."

He grinned at her, "Yeah, I really appreciated Maria and you having my back when I found out. I like working here."

"Maria has great respect for you, sees you going to the top. Trust me, we want to keep you happy." She changed the subject, "You didn't see anyone else on the beach last night?"

He frowned. "You know, I was upset so I wasn't paying much attention. Now that I think about it, I think maybe I heard someone running behind me and a splash. I didn't turn around." He looked down at his hands, clenching and unclenching them, "I wish I had."

"I wish you had too." Mia reassured him, "People play on the beach at night all the time. I walked on the beach for a few minutes before turning in for the night. There's no way to tell."

"Yeah," Francisco looked up as the police came back in the room.

"Okay, Mr. González, we've taken all your knives. I'm sorry for the inconvenience, but you should get them back quickly." He patted the worn leather bag. "We'll take care of them, don't worry. I want you proved innocent as quickly as possible so I can move on to the next suspect." He held up a clear evidence bag. "We've also taken your dirty clothes to test for blood stains. We will return those quickly as well."

Sergeant Waters handed Francisco a receipt, "Here's a list of everything we've taken to examine at the lab."

He scanned it and signed at the bottom. "I hope you catch whoever did this. I did not like Trey, but no one deserves to die like that."

"Oh, we'll catch them." The police started down the apartment stairs to their car, and Mia paused just long enough to pat Francisco on the arm.

"We'll visit Maria Sotos's house next," Danny told her. "Then we'll go to the main hotel."

"I think I'll skip Maria's house since Javier, her husband, is there. I have a few things I need to do back at the main hotel." She smiled ruefully, "I need to try to keep everyone from leaving."

"Need a lift?"

"No, you go on," Mia started walking down the main island road. She needed a few minutes to think. So much had happened in the past twenty four hours that she needed to consider.

After the police left, Francisco stood on the back porch, looking out at the tangle of leaves. The palmetto leaves scraped against each other, each louder than the next. Birds sang in the trees, and a bit of Spanish moss trailed from the porch railing. All the familiar sounds he'd gotten used to over the past few months were strange now. Suddenly, he felt lost in this foreign country, with his family so far away.

With a sudden breeze, salt air and the smell of hot sand came to him. He was suddenly back, a boy playing volleyball on the beach, sliding on hot sand. It didn't seem so long ago.

He'd worked so hard to be here, following his dream of being a chef in a great restaurant. Those days on the sand had been few and far between. He'd worked at least one job most summers and every afternoon after school. They hadn't been rich and they hadn't been poor, his family, but life had been a lot harder after his father had died. His father had left the insurance money, but his mother needed that to take care of his sisters.

He'd worked hard and gone to the best culinary school in the world with his own money. It had been worth it too, getting a job in the United States, where he could perfect his English and cooking skills at the same time. Someday, when he had the restaurant of his dreams, both of those skills would help him.

Trey had fired him, and now he was dead. It was terrifying, thinking of the crazy man coming after him, down the beach. More so to think of a murderer with a knife. Would he have been stabbed like Trey if he'd turned around at the wrong moment? He'd been so close to death and had never known a thing.

A bird screeched loudly in the tree above him, and he took a quick breath of salt air. He was here and alive. And Trey was dead.

He wondered just how crazy the murderer had been, after all. Trey was a sick bastard who liked screwing with other people's lives. He'd been mad at Francisco because last time he'd shown up at one of the girls' movie nights, Francisco had casually dropped by as well when Misty had texted him. Trey had punished him by firing him at the first excuse he found.

Francisco would never forget the avid glee he had seen in Trey's eyes when he had come into his kitchen, in front of Chef François, no less, and fired him. It had taken all of his self control not to punch that look out of Trey's face.

Francisco slowly breathed in the salt air. Trey was dead, and he'd never screw with another person's life again.

Danny knocked on Maria Sotos's front door and her teenage son answered, tall and gawky, his face surly. "Is your mom or dad here?"

Javier's usually cheerful face was drawn and tired. "Maria said you have to search our home," he said uncomfortably. "For the murder weapon."

"Yes, sir," Danny showed him as much respect as he could muster. The last thing he wanted was a nice man like Javier thinking the police were out to get him. Javier had coached his nephew's Little League two years ago, and Danny doubted he was capable of cold blooded murder. He strongly preferred that someone else, someone less rooted in the community was guilty. But he'd go where the evidence led him.

Javier opened the door wide to him and his sergeant. "Can I get you anything to drink?" he politely offered.

"No, sir," Danny replied, and Sergeant Waters demurred as well.

The house was nice, a little messy around the edges, with shoes in the front hall and mail on the table. Not quite a dishwasher load lay in the sink, waiting for the dishwasher to finish. The interior was painted in bright, happy colors. Big glass doors on the back flowed into the wraparound porch and backyard.

"You don't have to search my room, do you?" the teenager asked mutinously.

"We do," Danny told him gently. "We want to clear your mom of this crime."

"Or frame her," he accused.

Sergeant Waters made a quick move forward that Danny checked sharply.

His father quickly cut in, "Now Jake, that's not what he's doing."

"Your mom said you're going to be a lifeguard here this summer," Danny told him. "I used to lifeguard here too."

"You did?" Danny could see Jake slowly realizing he was human too. His bony arms relaxed toward his sides.

"Just like your dad too," he continued. "Now I'm police chief."

"Like that means anything," the kid scoffed, his face twisting.

"It means I try my very best to keep the streets safe. If someone commits a terrible crime like this murder, I try to catch the person who actually did it. There would be no point otherwise." Danny remembered being angry and afraid of authority, just like this kid. It didn't feel all that long ago either.

His father sighed, "Jake, he's on our side since we're innocent. We didn't kill anyone, and we want that proved as quickly as possible."

"We're going to search the house for a knife that could be a murder weapon. We'll probably take away a few kitchen knives and return them after they've tested negative for human blood."

Javier nodded agreement.

Danny continued, "The murderer would have gotten a lot of blood on them. We'll search for bloody clothes."

Javier nodded again, and Jake relaxed a little with the definite plan.

"Then let's get this over with," Danny told them.

He and Sergeant Waters searched the house thoroughly, but found nothing.

Mia walked along the Spanish moss shrouded path, enjoying the play of light and shadow on the oyster shell road. She considered the possible suspects in turn, discounting each.

She was worried about Javier's old trouble coming out and the effect it would have on Maria. She didn't know if Javier had even told his children about his past.

She couldn't imagine Maria killing Trey Sulley to keep him from telling what was on public record. She could absolutely see Maria defending her own life—or her son's life—against an armed attacker. There was only Maria's word for it that she hadn't met Trey Sulley on the beach. She still couldn't see Maria running away from anything, except to call an ambulance and police.

Maria had done an excellent job running the hotel for over a decade. She'd worked under Mia when she had first come to the hotel many years ago. Mia considered her a good friend. She thought Maria had made a mistake not firing Trey Sulley a long time ago, but he had come with such good references and... Mia stopped walking.

Why had he come with such good references? The St. Johns, San Francisco, was a five star, extremely formal hotel. From their brief acquaintance, she didn't see how Trey Sulley could possibly have met their standards. She made a note to check out those stellar references for possible blackmail victims. She wondered if maybe Trey had blackmailed someone there as well. A lot of things people didn't want the world to know about happened in hotels.

Who else? Well, Francisco. She didn't think Francisco was a murderer either. A Cordon Bleu graduate could get another job without much trouble, and she couldn't imagine the head chef badmouthing him. Any career setback would be temporary, unless there was something she didn't know.

Francisco might have defended his life if he'd been attacked, certainly. And from that photo and the timing, Trey had been coming after Francisco. He probably blamed Francisco for his dismissal.

Francisco was a Mexican citizen. He might have been nervous about calling foreign police, even working in the United States legally. Mia knew if she'd killed someone in self defense in a foreign country, she would call her lawyer first, then the foreign police. A scared kid might try to pretend it had never happened. She remembered her stepsons "forgetting" to tell her about relatively minor fiascos in the hope the problems would magically disappear.

Francisco seemed open and honest, but she didn't know him very well. She shook her head. She didn't want it to be him. She liked him.

Except for the additional scandal, she wouldn't mind the murderer being Hannah Winley. She was an unpleasant young woman who showed no signs of caring for others. She had been disturbed by Hannah's callous casting off of Phillip when he broke his ankle.

Hannah Winley certainly had motive, if Trey was a blackmailer. Undoubtedly millions of motives, if her husband found out about her little get away with her tennis pro. She'd probably be able to shrug off some of it, unless Trey had photos, which couldn't be that difficult to get. Hannah hadn't exactly been discrete.

Mia nodded to herself, Hannah was the most logical murderer. As well as, she thought with inner satisfaction, the person she'd most prefer to be a murderer. She'd find out more about any interactions the two had had. Now she had a plan to start with. She still had an entire hotel of possible suspects.

Still walking in deep thought, Billy startled her when he pulled one of the golf carts up across her path.

"Hop in, Ms. Mia," he told her, smile beaming across his wrinkled face. "You look all in."

"You know, you're right, Billy." She looked at her watch, "It's lunchtime, and it's already been a long day."

"Terrible thing to happen," Billy said. "I didn't like Sulley much, but a knife is a terrible way to go. It reminds me too much of overseas." Billy had seen too much violence after many years in the Marines.

"It is terrible," Mia agreed. "Any ideas on what happened?"

"All kinds of ideas, Ms. Mia, but no answers."

"How's the hotel looking? Lots of checkouts?" She hoped the murder wouldn't hurt the hotel. She knew the hotel had been around long enough to weather the long term, but she didn't know what would happen in the short term.

"Not as many as you'd think." Billy chuckled. "I think a lot of guests got free passes for fishing trips and boat rides though. I've maybe ferried thirty around the island so far this morning."

"Good," Mia was relieved.

"I think people see Trey's murder as a personal event, not a hotel event. After all, he wasn't even a guest."

"True, most people are here to relax and escape the real world. They probably don't care very much about a hotel employee dying. The hotel should weather this alright."

"Let's just not have another murder," Billy told her.

Mia decided to have lunch on the terrace overlooking the beach. The police had finished long ago and removed the police tape. The tide had come up and washed away Trey's blood. Most guests still chose to walk the other direction on the beach, but as she looked, one couple holding hands wandered past where Trey's body had lain so short a time ago. They didn't even glance at the murder spot, only at the gentle waves and each other.

Maria came by her table, perching uncomfortably on the edge of a chair to give her an update. "Everything seems okay, so far," she said hopefully.

"How many have left?" Mia wanted the bad news first.

"Ten so far. And eight cancellations."

"Not great, but not terrible, under the circumstances."

"I'm giving out free golf rounds, fishing trips, spa services and everything else I can think of. Sullivan has been great about matching the guests with an appropriate freebie."

"Good, let's keep our guests happy," Mia took a bite of her crisp salad dotted with chunks of seared tuna. It was perfect, with just a hint of spicy lemon. "Anything else I should know about?"

Maria gave a huge sigh. "Do you want me to resign now or after this mess is over? I'd like to clean up as much as I can before I leave, but I understand if you would like me to leave now."

Mia put down her fork and held her hand out across the white tablecloth, "Maria, I consider you a friend, no matter what." Maria grasped her hand and nodded agreement, tears in her eyes. "However, as you said earlier, Spinel Hotels employees do get several chances. In all your years with us, I don't think you've ever made even one before. This was a slight lapse in judgement, but you're an excellent hotel manager. I wouldn't dream of replacing you. Unless you'd like to move to headquarters in Atlanta?" she added wickedly.

Maria squeezed her hand and stood up, "In that case, I have things to do. This will remain the best hotel these guests have ever been to."

Mia smiled at Maria's fighting spirit and savored another bite of her salad.

It was a nice day for golf and boats and outdoor activities, she thought. Couples walked up and down the beach, enjoying the sun and sand. One or two hardy swimmers were out splashing in the cold surf.

She noticed the birdwatching couple, the Brownings, going into the water. The elderly couple were hand in hand, stoically entering the freezing water. They made it out to chest deep, then headed back for shore. "Brrr," Mia thought. It looked tropical, with palm trees and blue water, but it was far from warm this early in the season.

Harold Stone's assistant, Sylvie, walked up and down the beach, lost in thought. She seemed sad for such a beautiful day. Mia wondered what was wrong.

As she left, she passed Rebecca and Allison having lunch at the far end of the terrace, in the shade of an arbor. They were deep in conversation as she passed, but both smiled when Mia waved hello.

Allison seemed concerned, "I can't believe there was a murder here." She shook her head, "It just doesn't seem like the sort of place a murder could happen."

Rebecca said thoughtfully, "I think murders could happen anywhere people are. It just takes a murderer and a victim encountering each other." She looked around her at the beach and palm trees. "But you're right, it doesn't seem like a murder would happen in this peaceful paradise."

Mia waved goodbye, "Have a nice lunch, girls." She walked down the path to the Heron Building to meet the police.

As she'd thought, the hotel had provided the police with a nice buffet lunch. Sergeant Waters was just finishing a hearty salad with what looked like some of everything on offer piled high. She nodded stiffly to Mia.

Captain Daniels came to her, looking at his notebook. "Hello, Mia. Next on our list is Harold Stone. " He frowned, "He's quite a famous writer, so I don't want to bring his lawyers into a room search if he's innocent."

"No, I'd prefer it be kept quiet too, of course." She looked at him, "However, Harold Stone doesn't seem to prefer quiet. He had quite a loud argument with Trey about his laptop. At the time, I thought Trey had simply found the laptop where Harold had left it. Now...," she trailed off.

He looked at his notes. "It could go either way."

She said acidly, "He shows every sign of being an alcoholic so I think your reception will depend largely on what stage in the cycle he's in. I saw his assistant walking on the beach a few minutes ago so there's a good chance he's in his room. If not, Sullivan can find out his location quite easily."

"You keep that close track of your guests?" Sergeant Waters asked curiously.

"Oh, yes," Mia replied with certainty. "Besides security cameras monitoring the bridge, we have cameras at all the central locations and buildings."

Sergeant Waters said disapprovingly, "That seems like spying."

Mia said with decision, "After you've sent a search party out a few times for a guest hiking on the trail, twisting their ankle on the beach or lost in the marshy area, it became very nice to have an idea in what direction people were headed."

"Yeah, remember that lady that went hiking through the marsh and had her shoes sucked off by the mud? First one sandal, then the next." Danny said reminiscing. "It took almost all night to find her and was she scared!" He turned to his sergeant. "She was sure she'd seen an alligator after her so she climbed a tree. I practically had to peel her off of it."

"That was certainly a night to remember," Mia agreed. "Thank God for modern technology." She told

Sergeant Waters, "We erase all footage automatically after one week, so they couldn't be used for divorce cases or something we'd prefer the hotel not be associated with."

"Something Mrs. Winley should be thankful for," Captain Daniels added.

"What about this week's footage?" Sergeant Waters was concerned.

"If you like, I'll text Maria to check, but the protocol is if a crime is reported to the police, the rolling deletion skips until restarted."

"Do you have many crimes?"

"You'd probably know more than I would, but I think there was a car break in last year?" She looked at Danny. "Anything else?"

"That's about it," he confirmed. "We caught the guy right away, a bored teenager staying here." He looked disgusted, "His parents paid off the victim and hushed it up. Just a matter of time before he escalates to something they can't hush up." He looked sad at the waste, then cheered himself up, "At least he wasn't local so it won't be my problem."

They'd been striding along briskly while talking and made it to the main building. "Let's hope Mr. Stone will agree to the search. The more suspects off the list, the better."

"It's a pretty short list already," Sergeant Waters said doubtfully. "And not having blood or a knife doesn't exactly eliminate the suspect."

"No, but most criminals are pretty stupid," Captain Daniels reassured her. "Odds are we'll find the weapon or blood. Or information leading to a blackmail connection."

The Sergeant still looked doubtful, but went up the white stairs obediently.

Harold Stone's suite was on the third floor, accessed with a private elevator from the lobby. As she knocked at the door, Mia wondered how he would take the idea of a room search, but when she saw him, she realized he was in no shape to protest.

He blearily waved them around the room, seeming to think they were here to clean the room.

And did it need cleaning, Mia thought. If anything, it was in a worse state than Hannah Winley had left hers. He had failed to leave his lunch tray out for room service to pick up, and the remains lay shoved to the side on the coffee table. The table's surface was gashed where something had fallen on it. The curtains were drawn, and the room was dark in the middle of the day. His laptop was open at the small desk in the corner, but the screen was black and empty.

He'd clearly been watching television when they arrived, and a reality show rerun was still blaring at full volume, making it impossible to think.

"May I turn this off, Mr. Stone?" Sergeant Waters asked politely. Without waiting for his passive nod, she turned it off. He didn't seem to notice.

"Mr. Stone, as you probably know, Mr. Sulley was murdered last night. I'd like to ask you a few questions about your activities during the night."

"My activities?" He drunkenly winked at Sergeant Waters, "What about your nighttime activities?" He suddenly demanded, "Hey, who is Mr. Sulley? I don't know any Sulley."

Mia broke in, "The assistant manager, Mr. Trey Sulley. I believe you had some trouble with your laptop yesterday?"

"Oh, yeah. That guy." He wagged his finger at them, "That man was up to something. Stealing my stuff. No way I left my laptop in the lobby. No way."

"He found your laptop in the lobby?" Captain Daniels questioned.

"He pulled it out from under my chair," Harold Stone confirmed. He wagged his finger again, "I tell you there's no way I left it there. Sylvie, she's a good girl, she'll tell you." He looked around the darkened room. "Where'd Sylvie go? She'll tell you I never leave my laptop." He looked at them secretively, "It has my books on it, you know."

"May I ask what you were doing on the beach last night?"

"Was I on the beach last night?" He looked at them for guidance. "I might have gone for a walk?"

"You did go for a walk. We have a photo of you walking up the beach in the same direction as the murder."

"Really?" Harold was clearly surprised. "I don't remember." He racked his few functioning brain cells. "I think I would have remembered a dead body."

"One would hope so." Danny was clearly giving up on questioning the author. "Mr. Stone, may I search your suite for a knife or bloodstained garments?"

Harold signed the paper shoved at him with a drunken scrawl.

"Sure, sure, Sylvie will tell you where everything is." He peered at the drawn curtains like she might be hiding behind them. "She was here just a minute ago." His eyes lit up as he saw his laptop, "There's my laptop, see, in my room like it should be." He closed his eyes and leaned back, "Gonna just take a quick nap. Look at whatever. Nuthin to hide." His mouth gaped open hideously in a snore.

"Right," Captain Daniels went to work. "Nothing outside the scope of the murder weapon and bloodstain search. He's not in a state to agree to anything else, and frankly, I don't want to know."

Sergeant Waters moved efficiently through the putrid clothes with gloved hands, obviously trying not to breathe.

"They should issue you masks," Mia commented. She opened one curtain to look at the balcony. Items were scattered around the floor, so she went out the door, leaving it open for fresh air.

A book, some dishes from a previous meal, a bottle of Scotch lay forgotten. She prodded a pile of clothes with her foot, and saw some stains on a shirt. "Sergeant Waters," she called softly. "Tomato sauce or blood?"

"Could be either," she said, distastefully bagging them.

They continued the search, but that was all they found.

"Mr. Stone," Captain Daniels yelled a few times to wake him up. "Please sign a receipt for these items."

"Sure, sure," Harold's eyes drooped as he signed.

"Can you identify the stain on this shirt?" the police officer bellowed.

The drunk's eyes briefly flickered to the bagged shirt. "What's that? Oh, cut myself shaving. Yeah, shaving," he fell back asleep.

"Thank you for your cooperation, Mr. Stone," Captain Daniels said softly to deaf ears, as they closed the door.

"Hopefully, Mr. Stone's blood type will not be the same as Mr. Sulley's. If he did cut himself shaving, that will be a quick check for the lab."

"That's a lot of blood for shaving," Sergeant Waters commented.

"Ever shave drunk?" Captain Daniels said disgustedly. "Who else is in the hotel? Allison Jayton is the one you saw at Mr. Sulley's place?"

They knocked, but no one answered the door.

"That elderly couple then, Mr. and Mrs. Browning." Luckily, the Brownings were home. They opened the door to their room and welcomed the police in.

"The murder?" Mrs. Browning questioned. "Oh, yes, we heard about it. Terrible, terrible. We said at the time, didn't we, Harry," she looked to her husband for confirmation. "We must have been right near the murder. Absolutely terrifying."

She didn't look terrified. She looked like she'd missed a rare bird sighting, Mia thought.

There were bird books stacked on the credenza, several binoculars, cameras dwarfed by their white lenses and other birding equipment. It looked like they had gone to a birding store and bought one of everything.

The rest of the room was reasonably neat. A few jackets hung on chairs and drinks set neatly on coasters. High tech walking sticks leaned against one corner. Notebooks were laid out on the table along with an island map. They'd clearly been planning their next attack on Grand Island's bird population.

"You want to search our room for knives and bloodstains?" the elderly man said curiously.

"As you said, you were on the beach shortly before the murder. You didn't return to the hotel by the beach?"

"No, we went back by the main road to look for owls," Mr. Browning explained. "Do I need my lawyer?"

"You really want to search our room? Like in a murder mystery?" Mrs. Browning clearly had no problem with the search.

She looked at her husband, "Honey, just let them search. We don't have anything to hide, after all."

"I suppose," Mr. Browning was less confident in the police search but he acquiesced. "After all, we're right here."

Captain Daniels asked, "Did you see anything out of the ordinary last night? Something that might help us solve this murder?"

Mr. Browning said, "It's hard to remember. We've been owling a few nights since we've been here. We actually spotted a great horned owl and its mate last night."

"We've only been here a week," Mrs. Browning informed them.

"Yes, and we've been out two or three times. Last night... I think we saw the manager walking home. We definitely saw a great horned owl." He looked to his wife for confirmation. Clearly, Mr. Browning would have noticed a bird of any species, but humans were more difficult.

Captain Daniels nodded, "Yes, that's correct. Anyone else?"

"I just don't remember anyone in particular. I'll have to think on it. We're trying to find the owls' nesting site." He tapped a large scale map. "I think we have it narrowed down to a few possible locations."

"Please let me know if you think of anything to do with the murder of Trey Sulley."

"Of course."

Mia told them, "I'm Mia Spinel, with the hotel. I'm so sorry about the inconvenience. I hope your stay has been nice other than this brief interruption."

"We've added twenty birds each to our life lists," Mr. Browning informed her proudly. "That's a record week. If we can find that owl nest," he sighed in rapture.

"Have you taken a boat yet to Bar Island? That's usually a prime spot for interesting birds in the spring migration."

"Really?" Mr. Browning wasn't paying attention to the search anymore, though Mrs. Browning was watching the police carefully inspect their room like it was a Hollywood production put on just for her.

"Oh, yes," Mia had all the excursion information on tap still. "It takes about three hours total, and you should find quite a few interesting birds there this time of year.

If you tell the concierge I sent you, he'll set it up for free, as an apology for the trouble this has caused you." She waved her hands at the search.

They found no knives or blood. They left Mr. Browning thrilled at the boat trip and Mrs. Browning thrilled she'd been in a real live murder mystery. The last words they heard were, "I can't wait to tell Susie!"

"Well, at least we've made someone's day," Danny said wryly.

Sissy Collinsworth was in her room when they knocked and opened the door abruptly wide. "The police? Oh, that awful hotel manager who was killed. That's nothing to do with me."

Mia spoke up, "Ms. Collinsworth, I heard from Maria Sotos you had some trouble with Mr. Sulley, and I just wondered if you knew anything that might help the police?"

"Trouble with Mr. Sulley?" Sissy seemed confused.

"I just understood you preferred to deal with Mrs. Sotos, the manager," Mia told her.

"Well of course I did." Sissy said importantly. "Functions like mine, for the Green Environmental Charity, should always be handled on the highest level." Her eyes darted from one person to the other.

Captain Daniels conciliated, "Ah, I see." He nodded benevolently, "Since you did have contact with Mr. Sulley, may I search your room so I can cross you off my suspect list?"

"What are you searching for?" Sissy said belligerently.

119

"The knife Mr. Sulley was stabbed with and any bloodstained clothes," he said reasonably.

"I don't need my room searched by the Gestapo," Sissy said hostilely.

"Ma'am, we are police officers investigating a murder. We really don't want to have to come back with a search warrant," Captain Daniels told her calmly.

"If you want to search my room, you need a warrant!" Sissy slammed the door in their faces.

"Well, that's that for now," Captain Daniels said sadly. "It would have been nice to cross her off our list."

Sergeant Waters offered, "It's still a pretty slim chance the murderer would bring the weapon back to their room."

"True, but we have to search every part of the hotel."

This time when they knocked on Allison Jayton's door, she was in. "Just got back from biking," she cheerfully told them, still putting her hair up after a shower. "Gorgeous day!"

"It is a fine day for biking," Captain Daniels told her. "Unfortunately, we're here about something much more unpleasant. You know about Mr. Sulley's death?"

"Yes," Allison sobered. "Such a beautiful place for a murder to happen. This island has been heaven." She quizzed them, "What do you need from me?"

"You were seen coming out of Mr. Sulley's house at rather an early hour yesterday morning. May I ask what you were doing there?"

Allison blushed, "Oh, that was no big deal. We met early that morning during my run. He invited me to breakfast, and I thought it sounded like fun. I'm trying

120

to break out of my comfort zone a little. Make new friends."

"I see. Did you sleep with him yesterday morning?"

Allison said, "No, I...," she hesitated. "We just had breakfast. Eggs. That had obviously been his plan and I thought about it but - I just didn't know him that well yet."

Sergeant Waters asked in disbelief, "You weren't having an affair with him? You just went to breakfast at his house?" She clearly wasn't buying it.

Officer Daniels gave her a look and talked over her. "I see, Ms. Jayton. May we search your room for the murder weapon and any bloodstained clothes?"

"Oh, I don't know," Allison clearly wasn't sure, especially with Sergeant Waters glaring at her distrustfully.

Mia reassured her, "They've searched several other guests' and employees' rooms already. You're not being singled out. If you're innocent, it will help get you off their suspect list. If you're uncomfortable with it, just tell them to leave."

"Oh, okay," she agreed. "I guess I was alone with Trey so that puts me on the list?"

Captain Daniels nodded, "It's a long list."

"Of other women?" Allison looked disgusted.

"No, no," Mia told her. "People who had any close contact with Mr. Sulley."

"Okay." She opened the door, letting them in.

Allison's suite was messy, but not unduly so. Mia noticed all her clothes were new, with very couture labels. Quite a lot of makeup and treatment products were on her vanity table, which went with her plastic surgeries. No point in reconstructing your face if you didn't take care of it afterwards.

Allison looked steadily more uncomfortable at the police going through her things methodically. No drawer was unopened or dirty laundry unchecked. Even the stack of books on her bedside table was carefully checked.

Mia motioned to her, "Why don't we go out on the balcony and let them do their job alone?"

"Shouldn't I watch?" She eyed Sergeant Waters pawing her belongings distrustfully.

"No, don't worry," Mia soothed. "They're usually very quick."

They went out on the balcony, leaned on the railing and looked out at the waves. Allison Jayton had one of the prime rooms, where she overlooked the southern end of the island and the ocean.

Allison looked back at her room, "I never dreamed having breakfast with Trey would lead to this." She looked at the ocean view. "Thank goodness I didn't sleep with him. They'd be checking DNA and accusing me of murder."

"This is definitely outside the normal scope of vacation. Not something you can plan for." Mia stroked the railing with her hand, noticing an area the paint had flaked away. Probably time to repaint the railings. The ocean air was hard on paint.

"I mean, I didn't even like him that much, I just wanted - I don't know," Allison trailed off.

"It can be hard to be alone," Mia said. When Leo had first died, she'd tried to fill up the days so she didn't have to think. She had gradually realized she was the same person without Leo as with him. She'd moved on to enjoying both her current life and her memories. The first six months had been the hardest of her life.

"Yeah, I guess," Allison agreed. "I guess when I decide where I'm settling down, I'll make friends. Start really meeting people."

"Of course you will." Mia had always made friends wherever she was, but people were different. "Rebecca and you looked like you were having fun at lunch," she said cheerfully.

"Yes, she's really nice, isn't she?" Allison said. "We went biking around the island after lunch. I think we're meeting for a run tomorrow morning."

"That's great," Mia noticed Danny waving to them, "Why don't you have dinner with me tonight? I'll find out if Rebecca's free too." Rebecca and Sam might need an evening apart, from what she had seen. A girls night would be fun. Mia liked any excuse for a party.

"That would be fun," Allison agreed, her face brightening.

They headed back into the room. Sergeant Waters was standing stiff and erect, but her eyes were still searching corners.

"I'll see you at the Grand Palmettos Dining Room at eight o'clock then."

Mia and the police left to finish their searches.

"Find anything?"

"No, the only possible murder evidence is still Mr. Stone's shirt." He shook his head, "And I really do think it's extraordinarily bad shaving. Did you see the scabs on his face?"

Captain Daniels looked at his list, "Last one is Sam Forrest. He works for Spinel Hotels?"

"No, his wife, Rebecca, works in HR for Spinel in Atlanta. He has worked on a few cases for Spinel so I know him fairly well, but he's a partner in a separate law firm."

"Mr. Forrest?" Captain Daniels knocked firmly on the door.

Sam opened it, as if he'd been waiting for them. "Yes?"

The captain requested a search of the Forrests' room to look for the knife and bloodstained clothes.

Sam smiled hesitantly at Mia and ushered them in the door. "Sure, please look for anything you want." He looked around the room, as if wondering where to go.

"If you don't mind, Mr. Forrest, I'd like to ask you a few questions while my sergeant searches your room."

"Fine, fine," Sam motioned Captain Daniels and Mia to chairs, and he sat on the sofa where he'd clearly been sitting. "Rebecca's out biking now, should be back soon," he told Mia. "What do you need to know?"

"Mr. Forrest, what were you doing breaking into Mr. Sulley's house last night at approximately the time of the murder?" He drew out another photo, one Mia hadn't seen. It clearly showed Sam on Trey Sulley's front porch and was time stamped shortly after the earlier photo.

"No!" Mia nearly cried out, but held it in. Sam couldn't possibly be connected with Trey Sulley's murder. But breaking into Trey's house in the middle of the night?

Sam looked at the photo and sighed resignedly, instantly turning to stone. "I decline to answer on the grounds it might incriminate me," he stated firmly.

"That is your right," Captain Daniels said. "Are you sure you can't clear this up quickly?"

"I decline to answer," Sam repeated dully.

"You realize that gives me no choice but to take you in for questioning?" Captain Daniels told him. "Are you sure?"

"Yes, I'm sure," Sam stated.

"Did you even know Trey?" Mia blurted out.

"No, I didn't know him," Sam told her directly. "I can't answer any more questions without my lawyer."

"You are a lawyer," Mia muttered.

Sam smiled thinly. "Take care of Rebecca, okay, Mia?"

"Of course." She was surprised he even had to ask.

They sat there, wordless, while Sergeant Waters finished searching the rooms. "I found this tucked under the mattress," she showed them a laptop. "There are two other laptops on the table, looks like his and his spouse's."

"Is this your laptop or your wife's, Mr. Forrest?"

Sam stared straight ahead.

"All right, have it your way." He told Sergeant Waters, "Bag the laptop. I'll take him down to the station."

He pulled out handcuffs, and Mia winced as she heard the metal links clink. Danny saw her face. "Will you come quietly, sir?"

Sam nodded agreement, and Danny put the handcuffs back. "Let's go."

Mia followed the dismal trio down the hall. The elevator arrived, and Rebecca came out glowing with energy after her bike ride. She saw Sam and the police, and her face went white, then crumpled, all joy gone.

Mia reached around the police, and pulled Rebecca out of their way, dragging the much larger woman down the hall back to their room, like a tugboat and a cruise liner. She ordered her, "Rebecca, don't say a word until we get to your room."

Rebecca tried to speak and Mia tugged hard at her. "Let's get you out of this, right now. I'll tell you."

Sam's eyes thanked her as she glanced back. The sound of the elevator doors quietly closing like the gates of hell panicked Rebecca, and she tried to get back to Sam. Mia shoved Rebecca in the room and shut the door. Rebecca gave up, tears in her eyes.

She went over to the sofa and carefully sat down as if she might break. "Tell me," she said.

And Mia did.

5

Whodunit?

Mia tucked Rebecca in that evening after she had watched her eat every bite of a hearty bowl of soup. When Mia left to dress for dinner, Rebecca was already drowsy from a sleeping pill.

Her dinner that night took on new meaning. She was going to quiz Allison Jayton on absolutely everything she'd talked about with Trey that morning. Mia was going to look at, yes, she'd call them her suspects, and figure out which of them had killed Trey.

Because there was no way in the world Sam had killed Trey Sulley, no matter what. She didn't believe it for a minute, even if he had broken into Trey's house. Unfortunately, she did have to believe Sam had broken into Trey's house since that was clearly on video, and she guessed Trey's laptop was the one hidden under Sam's bed. Not good. Not good at all, she thought.

Mia dressed in more of a hurry than usual, pairing some of her more impressive jewelry with a deceptively simple dupioni silk blue dress. She had a feeling Allison would be impressed with expensive accessories. She brushed her hair, her natural waves falling into place as if they'd been trained to, which of course they had. Unlike her normal dinner heels, she wore flat shoes, since she planned to look at the lighting and security cameras on the beach at night, and didn't want to change after dinner.

Outside the restaurant, she greeted a very subdued Sullivan. "How are you?"

He looked awful, brittle smile pasted to his face and exhausted eyes. "I'm ok. My shift ends in a few minutes and I'm going home to collapse. I finally convinced Dorrie to take the afternoon off. She was all in."

"Good," Mia agreed. She leaned closer, "Any ideas on the murder?"

"There's no way Sam Forrest murdered anyone," Sullivan stated flatly. "I'm keeping my eyes and ears open. I'll let you know." He hesitated, "The gossip is Trey was blackmailing Sam." He watched her carefully for a reaction.

"You know about him trying to blackmail Maria." Mia offered, "I would guess blackmail had something to do with his murder."

"And I wondered if the glitch in the key card system might have something to do with blackmail."

Mia looked around. No one was close enough to hear. "That makes sense."

"The key cards and the room safes that people put their laptops and valuables in are tied to the same system. That way, they can be changed with the individual guest. Trey had access to rooms with his master key card, but not the room safes."

"It leaves both systems vulnerable at the same time." Mia wrote a quick note. "I wonder if the police have checked out those logs?"

"I haven't heard them request them." Sullivan looked hopefully at her, "Any suspects I should keep an eye on?"

"I'm still finding out more about Trey." Mia thought a minute, "I think Hannah Winley and Harold Stone were vulnerable from the blackmail angle. I'm curious whether Harold left his room last night. The keycard would show it?"

"I'll have security print logs for the police and a second copy for you."

"Thanks," Mia said.

"I'll keep an eye on those two then," Sullivan told her. "Just tell me if there's anyone else."

"I'm sure there will be. I hope Allison Jayton, who I'm having dinner with, might have some ideas, since she was friendly with Trey."

Mia noticed Allison descending the stairs and waved. "I'll see you tomorrow, Sullivan."

He nodded, and efficiently started looking through his computer. Concierges always knew everything about a hotel, Mia thought.

Allison wore a sleek black dress falling almost to her ankles with a long slit on the side that showed her stunning legs. Mia thought she recognized it from a Paris designer's recent collection. Allison had money to spend and a dramatic sense of style. She came down the stairs with the sense of making an entrance, and heads turned to see her walk down the red carpet.

Mia wondered how a woman with so much going for her could be lonely.

Allison greeted her, "I heard about Rebecca's husband being arrested for Trey's murder. I'm so sorry for her. How is she holding up?"

"She's okay, under the circumstances. I made sure she ate dinner, and she's sleeping now." Mia paused, "But Sam Forrest hasn't been arrested for the murder, you know. I really can't believe Sam would possibly do such a thing. I've known him for years. He's just being a typical lawyer, refusing to answer questions without his attorney."

"Oh, I see," Allison nodded, politely not contradicting Mia, though her eyes were disbelieving. "Well, that's good."

They walked into the dining room, Allison tall and dramatic in her black and Mia a foot shorter in her soft blue dress that matched the room. The headwaiter expectantly awaited his treasured guest.

"Just my usual table, Bernard," Mia said.

"Of course, Ms. Mia," he said, ushering them with proud care through his elegant domain. "I heard about Mrs. Forrest's husband. I do hope she isn't taking it too hard."

"Rebecca will be fine," Mia told him. "Sam is just refusing to talk without his lawyer."

"I'm very pleased to hear that," Bernard said with dignified relief. "Mrs. Forrest is always a great favorite with our team here."

"Do they come often?"

"I believe they visit almost every year, since it is so close to Atlanta. Naturally, they usually bring their children, and they have a very different kind of trip. I believe this is the first trip to the island on their own since they had children."

With a heartfelt sigh, Bernard resumed his professional demeanor, "May I bring you some of our crab cakes to begin?"

"And champagne as well, Bernard."

"But of course, Ms. Mia," the headwaiter looked shocked she even had to ask.

The small plates were set in front of them a few moments later by the headwaiter himself, beaming proudly. When Mia took a bite of the tiny crab cake, the crisp outside broke way perfectly to creamy crab inside. She savored every bite, realizing just how hungry she was after the long day.

"This is so worth my morning run," Allison gushed.

"I generally let Bernard tell me what to eat when I'm here," Mia beamed at him. "He's always right." The headwaiter bustled away, looking gratified.

When she smelled the bouillabaisse Bernard chose for them next, Mia was in heaven. The rich stew was a perfect melding of seafood, with crisp French bread and a spicy aioli sauce. The white Bordeaux chosen by the sommelier enhanced it beautifully.

After she took the edge off of her hunger, Mia let her eyes explore the room. The blue velvet draperies were drawn, and the candlelight made the grand room sparkle with a soft glow. Something seemed a little off today, but maybe it was just her.

The wedding parties had left after the ceremonies were performed, and the room wasn't as full as usual. The grand piano still played soft classical music in the background, but it grated in her present mood.

Allison nodded at Hannah Winley, "Looks like she has company tonight."

Two men, dressed in formal business suits, bookended the glittering blonde. They ate the delicious food mechanically, barely speaking. They were obviously there on business. Hannah did not look pleased to have them there. Her toothy smile never came near her eyes.

"Hmm, I wonder who they are," Mia mused.

"I imagine her husband's lawyers," Allison said dryly. "Of course."

"I wonder about her prenup," Allison speculated.

"I expect it will show up in headlines eventually."

"Do you think she murdered Trey? They had dinner together last night," Allison said eagerly.

"I don't know," Mia said. "Who do you think killed him?" she asked bluntly.

"I wish I knew." Allison shivered. "It's so weird, we had a nice breakfast together that morning, I waved hello to him a few times during the day, then he was dead by the next morning."

"It was very sudden," Mia agreed. "Did he seem scared of anyone?"

"No, he laughed a bit at Hannah Winley, said her husband was going to find out about her boy toy." She looked at Hannah, "I wonder if he was planning on telling her husband about her affair."

"I wouldn't be surprised," Mia sniffed. "Did he mention anyone else?"

"Not really. He was thrilled Harold Stone was staying here, said he couldn't wait to read his latest book and maybe he'd get to read it before anyone else." Allison smiled. "I was surprised since he didn't seem much of a reader. I didn't hear him say anything about the Forrests," Allison played with her forks, switching the shiny silver from spoon to dessert fork, back and forth.

"Trey lived in San Francisco last, like you," Mia told her.

"Really?" Allison looked surprised. "He never said. I thought he was from near here."

"He'd only been working here for a few months. He was at the St. Johns in San Francisco before that."

"Really?" Allison played with the forks more, "I've never been there."

"Oh, it's a lovely hotel," Mia said. "The most wonderful afternoon tea outside London."

"If I go back, I'll have to try it," Allison said, moving the shiny forks around, positioning them precisely by her plate. "I'm not sure when or if I'll go back there."

"There are so many places for you to go," Mia soothed. "Are you still thinking of moving to this area?"

133

"Yes, maybe Charleston or Savannah. Outside a city, but near an airport. I want to stay in the United States, but I like to travel."

"Do you travel often?"

"I love shopping in Paris," Allison enthused. "It's so much fun to buy dresses like this one," she smoothed the black silk down, "I had only seen in magazines. And the adorable little shops."

"There's nothing quite like shopping in Paris, is there? Those little shops down tiny streets have things like nothing else in the world," Mia reminisced. "Whenever I go to Paris, I always ask friends where the new treasures can be found."

"In college, I spent my year abroad in Paris. I would just wander around for hours and explore. I love the unique little shops like umbrella shops or lingerie shops. I found a tiny hat shop once you literally had to step outside the store to try on a hat. There just wasn't room inside." Allison mimed trying on a huge hat. "And the odd bookstores with random stairs to add a few more shelves. I could spend hours in those."

"I have to admit I love the brocante too. You just never know what you might find, from silk scarves to vintage dresses. I think I've picked up some of my favorite accessories at the Paris flea markets."

"And the food in every restaurant," Allison gushed. "I never can decide my favorite."

"It would be absolutely impossible to decide."

They looked around the room and Allison commented, "Looks like Harold Stone's assistant doesn't have a favorite part of her job."

"You know, I love his books, but how can someone that annoying write such meaningful stories?" Mia looked at Sylvie Summers, dining alone, and said impulsively, "Let's ask her to join us for dessert."

Allison nodded agreement.

Mia went over to Sylvie's table, where she sat finishing her main course. "Hello, I'm Mia Spinel, one of the hotel owners. We haven't been introduced, but I was told you're Ms. Summers, Harold Stone's assistant. We noticed you were dining alone tonight. We're just thinking of ordering dessert and wondered if you'd join us?" Mia said convivially.

The assistant looked up, startled. She had been lost in her own world, eyes shrouded behind large glasses. "Oh, I don't know..." she broke off with a shy smile, "you know, I'd love to." She hesitantly came over to their table. "Please, call me Sylvie."

"And I'm Allison."

"We're letting Bernard, the headwaiter, surprise us with each course," Mia told her with a smile, pouring her champagne in the glass Bernard had made magically appear. "He always comes up with the most fabulous menus."

"What fun," Sylvie said merrily. "I always have trouble deciding what to choose."

"And the headwaiter knows his own menu the best." Mia never had trouble deciding, but she always loved trying new options under expert advice.

Dishes of vanilla ice cream topped with large pecan pralines were placed before them. Allison said, after savoring her first bite, "Of course, Paris is amazing but the food in the United States can be pretty darn good."

"I've always thought lowcountry cuisine was some of the best in the world. It takes elements from so many great food traditions, like African and French, and merges them into something perfect."

"Mmm," Sylvie said, savoring her praline. "I never would have thought to order this on my own and it's absolutely delicious."

"I've always felt trying all the dishes at the hotel restaurants is one of my most important—and favorite—jobs," Mia said cheerfully.

"I don't think I've seen Harold eat anything but steak," Sylvie was relaxing with her glass of bubbly. "Never a green vegetable."

"Men skip vegetables so often," Allison agreed. "It can't be healthy."

"The problem is, so many people learned vegetables taste bad when they ate them as children. Parents would follow healthy eating guides, and boil or steam them with no salt." Mia lectured, "That is just not the way to make kids eat them." She smiled, "I never tried to hide vegetables from my kids. I just made them taste good. Salt and olive oil and butter. Yum."

"I still prefer ice cream," Allison admitted.

"I should learn to cook," Sylvie said dreamily, scraping her bowl for the very last bit of ice cream.

"Take a class," Mia suggested. "I always take them when I like the local cuisine."

"You should offer a cooking class at this hotel," Sylvie said. "I'd take it, if I could afford to."

"With how that man treats you, you should get paid enough to take any class you want," Allison said. "I know his books must make enough."

"Yes, well," Sylvie pushed her last praline around in her bowl, avoiding answering, eyes darting around the room. "Gosh, she doesn't look happy."

Hannah Winley stood up and threw the contents of her water glass into one lawyer's face. "Like hell I will," she screeched, like a petulant two year old. She stomped off in her four inch heels in the suddenly silent restaurant.

"Okay—," Allison commented. "I wonder what that's about."

"I wish people wouldn't argue in public," Mia disapproved.

"I hate scenes," Sylvie agreed. "Like when Harold screamed down the hotel over that stupid laptop." She suppressed a shudder, "That was awful."

"It must have been," Mia said sympathetically. "And he'd just left it in the lobby all along."

Sylvie frowned, "That was just so weird. I always check if he's left anything since he's usually," she stumbled, "not quite himself."

"Drunk," Allison supplied.

Sylvie said nothing, eyes clouded.

Mia soothed, "It's all right, dear, everyone knows. It's not exactly a secret when he insists on getting drunk in the hotel lobby." She went on, "You had checked his things?"

"Yes, but then that manager, the one who was killed, found it there." Sylvie shook her head. "I don't know, maybe I missed it," she concluded uncertainly.

"It's always difficult to remember things after an event," Mia told her reassuringly. Personally, she'd bet Trey had stolen it. She pushed back her chair smoothly. "Thank you both for lovely company tonight."

"Thank you so much for asking me for dessert. That was delicious," Sylvie said politely, like a well brought up child displaying her manners.

"We should definitely have a little dinner party this week," Mia said cheerfully. "Meeting new friends is one of the best things about travel."

Mia passed Hannah heading into the lounge from outside. She clomped by in her towering Manolo Blahnik heels, still obviously mad, and a few more sheets to the wind.

Mia followed the tipsy woman into the bar. She asked while perching on a stool, "May I join you?" She motioned for the bartender to pour a champagne for her.

"Yeah, sure," Hannah said grudgingly. "I ran out of Scotch at my cottage. Damn lawyers." She looked at herself in the bar mirror, leaning to see between the bottles.

"Having a rough night?" Mia asked kindly. She looked rough, Mia thought. She'd looked pretty bad this morning, with her makeup running down her face, but tonight she looked like she'd aged ten more years under the heavy makeup.

"Yeah," Hannah said, tears welling, smoothing her hair and checking her reflected image. "I shouldn't have signed that stupid prenup. Art would have married me anyway."

"I'm sure he would have." Mia doubted it. From what she'd heard of Arthur Winley, he was no fool. Not great taste in his wives, but very good lawyers.

"Yeah, lawyers mess everything up. Stupid prenup."

"Lawyers do cause trouble sometimes," Mia agreed. Or prevent it, she privately thought.

"I have to find money," Hannah whined. "I can't make it without money."

"It is a problem," Mia agreed again. She noticed Sissy Collinsworth glaring at her in the bar mirror. She was nursing a brandy in the corner, and looked planted for the night.

Hannah was still babbling drunkenly, "Trey was such scum, I don't know why the hotel had him here." She dimly focused on Sissy in the mirror. "Hey, Trey was asking you for money too," she called out, turning to point at her.

Mia looked at Sissy. Interesting. Sissy hurriedly got up and left the bar, brandy glass still in hand.

Hannah turned back to her reflection. "Asking me for money. Like I have money to give him." Hannah gulped her Scotch and held out the glass for more. "I need money," she demanded shrilly.

"I hope Trey didn't bother you too much," Mia said smoothly.

"No, no, took care of him," sputtered Hannah into her drink. "No problem. He didn't ask for more money." She looked at her empty glass, "I don't have money. I need money."

Mia said, feeling her way, "I'm glad Trey didn't ask for more money."

"No, no, he was dead. So no more money from me," Hannah said proudly.

"That's good."

Hannah leaned in to tell her with fetid breath, "I'll have a lot more money now that he's dead."

"That's nice," Mia leaned away distastefully.

"Yes, lots of money," she babbled drunkenly. She was losing coherence. After a few more conversations revolving around money, she settled into staring at herself in the mirrored bar, primping her hair.

Mia thought that was a good time to leave. She hoped Hannah didn't make a scene, but she knew the bartenders could deal with anything Hannah started, as well as carry her to her bed. Not the type of young woman she admired. And it sounded like she possibly was a murderer. Mia had to admit she'd much prefer Hannah to be the murderer than Sam.

Outside, the air was crisp and cool, wind blowing in from the sea. They purposefully kept lighting minimal away from the main terrace. People enjoyed walking on the dark beach at night, with only the stars for company. They could see enough light to guide them back to the hotel—and that was all that was needed. The paths between buildings had low lights to prevent tripping, but not enough to ruin the evening experience. A guest wandering on the side paths at night could probably avoid all security cameras if they had planned their route during the day.

While Hannah was still drinking, Mia walked around Palmetto Bluffs Cottage. It was the most isolated cottage, almost designed for clandestine entrances and exits. It probably had been, thought Mia. This cottage hadn't been built when she was manager, but there were always plenty of guests who strongly preferred their privacy, for various reasons.

The cottage's side furthest from the main hotel had thick palmetto scrub almost to the building, with dark unofficial paths leading directly to the beach and back to the road. The cute little front porch with its door didn't even have a railing preventing a direct exit to the dark beach path. The security camera was aimed at the area around the beach, not at the cottage. It would be easy enough to go past it on the unofficial path from the cottage.

Mia slowly walked down to the beach by the main path, trying to spot the security cameras. They really didn't have many, she thought. The bridge leading to the island was private, and the hotel kept a close watch on the cameras there. Anything going over the bridge triggered a signal in the security room. The guard on duty could immediately check if the newcomer was a legitimate visitor. During the crowded summer season or for special events, they stationed a guard to check people on and off the island.

The boat dock was another entry point to the island. That was another place they kept a close eye on security, but for the most part, once you were on the island, you were left alone.

Occasionally important guests would bring their own security, or Hollywood stars would request no press on the island. The Spinel Grand Island accommodated special requests as much as they could, placing extra guards on duty when needed. But now, in the off season, there was no need for that extra level of care. There were no celebrities with crowds of paparazzi hounding them. It was just a quiet, luxurious island hotel.

Once you were on the island, cameras were only at main roads and buildings, with just a few others placed around so they could find lost guests or identify problems. However, guests came here not just for luxury in the middle of beautiful natural scenery, but for peace and privacy. The hotel had no desire to intrude on honeymooning couples or people taking private strolls. Just to know what direction they were headed in case they got lost.

Which was all very well for privacy, Mia thought, but lousy for catching a cold blooded murderer. She guessed both Harold Stone and Hannah Winley were being blackmailed. After talking to Sylvie tonight, she could make a shrewd guess what Harold was being blackmailed about, but she didn't even have to guess what Trey might blackmail Hannah for. Frankly, Hannah was as obvious a philanderer as she'd ever seen.

The millions she might lose if her affair was documented were an excellent motive for Trey Sulley's

murder. Mia admitted to herself, she thought Hannah
was her prime suspect for the murder. Hannah seemed
the sort that might stab a man in the heart.

Mia walked up the beach to where the murder had
happened. She knew nothing was left of the blood, but
in the half light of the moon, every puddle in the sand
looked disturbingly dark. There were several paths
through the shrubby dunes leading to the center of the
island. Hannah's cottage linked up quite easily with one
of these. It was probably her preferred, private route to
the beach. It would be easy to lie in wait for a man to
walk past with an easy escape back to her cottage.

Footprints would be the only clue left. How many
times had Hannah and others walked on that same path
this week alone? Footprints would prove nothing.

Mia walked slowly back along the beach, looking up
at the hotel. There were the grand stairs to the main
hotel building, ending in two levels of well lit terraces
topped with stone balusters. The beach in front of the
main stairs was very well lit, meant to be enjoyed by
guests who might want to walk on the beach but were
wary of twisting an ankle. There were side paths
everywhere, places for honeymooning couples to stroll,
and small nooks for friends to have a quiet chat.

All in all, the Spinel Grand Island Hotel was an
ideal place to murder someone. Mia went back to her
quiet cottage and locked the door.

Sam got out of the taxi at the hotel entrance, and just stood there a minute. The last thing he felt like doing was going inside after the day spent at the suffocating police station. He looked up at the night sky. The stars were blotted out by the glare of the hotel lights. What he really wanted to do was go down to the beach and look at the stars in the cool night air.

He circled the grand building with its wide sweeping porches. In the daylight it resembled a white wedding cake, all frosting and curlicues. Tonight, it felt like a gothic horror movie, the outdoor lights making deep moving shadows under every balcony and awning. He hurried past dark palmettos clacking their brittle fronds, towards the beach. The long stone terrace glared with lights. He walked past the imposing main stairs and down a darker side path, palmetto shadows weaving into the curving path.

The sand felt softly slick on the leather soled shoes he'd worn to the police station. He padded uncomfortably up the dark beach. Away from the hotel lights, Sam finally saw the stars, brilliant lights scattered on the ink blue sky. He breathed in the salty night air. He could feel his breathing start to slow and his heart unclench.

It was beautiful here, on the island. He loved the ocean. He'd grown up not too far from the Sea Islands, outside Charleston. As a kid, he'd sailed a tiny sailboat, its battered hull already several generations old, around the salt marshes, fishing and playing with the other kids at the edge of the sea. He hadn't been sailing in over a year with his kids.

He thought of his own kids, safely at home, away from the news. He and Rebecca had called and told them how much fun they were having.

He suddenly wanted, more than anything, to take his kids sailing. Go play together in the surf.

Work had been hard lately. He'd thought his goal was making partner. He'd have a good job, and all the hard work would pay off. He hadn't expected the extra work to be quadrupled. And then Trey blackmailed him.

Looking out into the endless night, Sam hated Trey Sulley still, with all his heart.

He shook his head, neck cordoned tight. No point in that, now. It was all over. Trey Sulley was dead and gone.

Ahead in the dim moonlight, he saw the hippie woman standing where the police tape had blocked off the sand this morning. Her skirts pooled in the ocean. Her hands spread wide to the moon, she called to the night sky.

Sam abruptly turned, moving away from the woman. He saw shadows moving quickly where palmetto scrub met the rolling beach dunes. Deer or people, he wondered, peering into the night. Shadows seemed to leap in the distance as the palm trees swayed in the wind. An owl hooted in the distance, like a foghorn. A chill crawled down his back.

A murderer had walked on this beach last night, while he was here.

He walked quicker up the beach, slippery shoes fighting the sand sliding under his feet. He didn't look at the ocean now, but sent quick, anxious glances to the dunes. Shadows were tricky in the half light. Things seemed to move and change before his eyes.

He saw a running shape dart to the edge of the dunes and pause, seeming to look out at the woman calling to the moon. He squinted, something was definitely there, but animal or human? Before he could tell, it had left, merging into the shadows.

He walked up the stairs and felt eyes on his back, watching him go. He quickly turned around and saw nothing but the palmettos rattling their dead leaves. He heard creatures scratching in the leaf litter, turning over the sand like an hourglass.

Warm light shown in one of the cottages, that rich bimbo's, maybe. She must still be awake. A gust of wind blew hard, sending the shadows dancing, and he thought he saw someone leaving her porch. He wasn't surprised.

The oyster shell path scrunched under his feet, broadcasting his location. Like a hunted animal, he tried to quiet his footsteps, but every step seemed louder. The wind blew wildly behind him now. It chilled his bones.

He got to the brightly lit terrace with a feeling of relief at the same time, as the birdwatching couple walked off a side path. They were festooned with night vision goggles, spotting scopes and more equipment than they could possibly use attached to matching vests.

Sam breathed out with a sense of anticlimax. He'd let his imagination get the better of him, out on the beach. No wonder, after the day he'd had.

He politely held open the door for the elderly couple. As they navigated the door opening too small for their bulky equipment, he picked up her hiking stick.

Only Sam's quick reactions saved their professional looking spotting scope from crashing to the stone floor. They thanked him, night vision goggles still perched on their heads like a bizarre seal team.

He smiled and went to bed.

6

Sam's Story

On the morning, Mia woke to a phone call and Sam's voice. "I was released late last night after my lawyer got there, and I gave my statement to the police. Rebecca asked me to discuss it with you over breakfast."

"Of course, Sam. I'll see you both here in an hour." Mia quickly dressed in neat white pants and a blue and white tunic. She carefully put on bright pink lipstick and felt ready to face the day.

Dorrie was cheerfully setting the round table on the private patio with sparkling silver and crystal glasses. "Always nice to enjoy breakfast outside, isn't it, Ms. Mia?" Her black hair swung happily as her light steps danced around the table.

"It's a gorgeous day too." Mia felt happy and free in the crisp morning air. The tiny courtyard had high tabby walls surrounding, crowned with oyster shell decorations in a fan shape. "Sam and Rebecca Forrest are joining me for breakfast."

"Oh, good," Dorrie paused in her tasks. "Mrs. Forrest is such a nice lady. Those kids of hers are polite, too, unlike some."

"I'm so sorry you had to find Mr. Sulley's body, Dorrie. I'm glad you took the afternoon off after the shock," Mia said sympathetically.

"I've never seen anyone dead before," Dorrie said, remembering. "It was awful." She cocked her head to the side, considering, "I didn't like him much, but I wish he'd just left when he was fired."

"Yes, he would have been some other hotel's problem in two weeks. I wish he'd waited until then to be killed," Mia said. "Why didn't you like him?'

"Oh, he made passes at every woman he saw. He'd show up drunk at our doors and try to get in. We couldn't have a movie night without him insisting on coming in. Just creepy," she fiddled with a knife and straightened a crystal butter dish.

"I wish you'd told Mrs. Sotos," Mia said. "He would have been gone immediately."

"Yeah, it also just didn't seem like that big a deal, you know? There's always someone like that, and I like the hotel."

"I'm glad," Mia told her. "We think Trey was blackmailing people."

"Yeah, I heard."

Mia wasn't surprised the rumor had spread, "Did you see any evidence of that?"

Dorrie shook her head, putting out a silver basket of biscuits nestled in a white napkin. "It's hard to tell, you know?" She looked at Mia sideways. "I mean, every woman in the place, he tried to get close to. He sucked up to Mrs. Forrest, I know. Bringing her drinks and stuff she hadn't asked for when she was on the beach. He knew she was HR so probably hoped to get Mrs. Sotos's job by being nice to her."

"That makes sense," Mia agreed. "Not that it'd work."

Dorrie went on, more confidently, "And Mrs. Winley. He was totally after Mrs. Winley. She was here with that gorgeous Phillip guy, and Trey was still totally making passes at her. When I delivered room service to her cottage one time, I saw him peeping in the windows."

"No!" Mia said, outraged.

"Absolutely. He was a nasty peeping tom," Dorrie assured her with disgust.

"Did he have a camera?" Mia asked curiously. "He might have been after blackmail photos."

"Ohhh, you think that was it?" Dorrie shook her head, "I didn't see one, but everyone has a phone so..."

"Interesting. Who else was he targeting?"

"He was definitely sucking up to Harold Stone's assistant and frankly," Dorrie shook her head disparagingly, "that couldn't have been about her looks."

"No, she's a nice woman though," Mia said.

"Yeah, I guess. She's always got her head down like she's hiding behind her hair." Dorrie smiled with the superiority of age, "Reminds me of when I was a teenager."

Mia smiled. That couldn't have been so very long ago.

"How about the Brownings?"

"The birdwatching couple? No, I never saw them with Trey." Dorrie thought, "Trey and Harold Stone had that blowup the night before he was killed," she offered. "Mr. Stone is a nasty drunk."

"Yes, I noticed," Mia said dryly. "Another candidate for most likely to be a murderer then."

Dorrie laughed, "I'll try to think of some more unpleasant people for suspects then."

"Absolutely," Mia smiled.

Dorrie finished setting the table, and left in a much better mood.

Sam and Rebecca arrived as Dorrie left, walking past the room service cart, and nodding hello. She waved cheerily back and went on her way.

They both looked gray and exhausted. "Hi, Mia," Rebecca said without her usual bounce.

"Hello," Mia said cheerfully. "Perfect timing. Let's eat!"

The flaky biscuits smelled warm and buttery, and the eggs were done to perfection. A truly impressive feat for room service. The setting in the little courtyard was beautiful, with the distant sound of waves accompanying their meal. It wasn't the chef's fault the food didn't seem as delicious as usual. Sam and Rebecca ate almost mechanically, putting food in their mouths to prepare for their day.

Mia finally gave in and broke the silence, "Tell me about it."

Sam carefully put down his biscuit, patted his mouth with a napkin and took a long drink of water.

Rebecca cut in before he had a chance to talk, "Sam didn't kill Trey Sulley."

"No, of course not," Mia agreed. "Just let him tell his story, ok, Rebecca?"

"Ok," Rebecca sullenly spread marmalade on a biscuit and bit it vindictively.

"As Rebecca says," Sam began precisely, "I did not kill Mr. Sulley." He looked down at the white tablecloth and back up at Mia, "I am, however, guilty of breaking into Mr. Sulley's house."

"But why?"

"Mr. Sulley took advantage of a brief walk I made the day before to break into my room and copy confidential client information off my laptop, which was locked in the room safe." Sam sighed heavily. "I thought the simplest thing to do was recover the information and my client would be protected."

"I see," Mia said, shocked.

"And he didn't say a thing about it to me," Rebecca said, crumbling her biscuit.

"I didn't want you involved in what amounted to a robbery at what was, de facto, your place of employment," Sam told her dispiritedly. "That would have been highly unethical."

"Have you explained to the police?"

"Yes," Sam assured her. "I needed my lawyer to draw up an agreement that no information I gave unrelated to the murder would become public record." He smiled grimly, "I also didn't want to be disbarred for protecting my client against a blackmailing thief."

"Danny agreed to that?"

"Yes," Sam said in relief. "Thank God he did. However, he still thinks I'm a prime suspect, and I have to say I rather agree with his viewpoint." He said determinedly, "I know I'm not a murderer, but there's no reason why he should."

"Danny's always been a smart kid," Mia reassured him. "He's not going to rush to judgment."

"Good," Sam said, helping himself to another biscuit with more appetite, done with his story.

Mia wasn't letting him off quite that fast.

"So the information was on the hidden laptop?"

Sam put down his biscuit meticulously. "Yes, I had found the laptop, removed the hard drive and tossed it off the pier. I thought the salt water would destroy it, and I was correct, the police found. I did the same to a thumb drive that did have my client information on it." He shook his head, "Obviously, I wouldn't have done that if I'd known he was about to be murdered, and my client's information would be safe. I'm not exactly a computer hacker. I've just replaced a hard drive on my laptop so I knew how to do that." He sighed, "Frankly, I didn't really care if he could make it work again, after his little blackmail attempt. I thought I was doing a public service for anyone else who might be on his hit list."

"I would have done the same thing," Mia commiserated. "But I suppose the police weren't thrilled."

"No, he didn't back up to a cloud or anything. Good news for me, but not for their crime solving." He looked directly at Mia, "The only thing that will get me out from suspicion is if the murderer is found."

"Then that's what we have to do," Mia said emphatically.

As they were finishing breakfast, Dorrie ran in, "Ms. Mia! Come quickly! They can't wake Mrs. Winley up." She stopped, hunting for breath, then whispered hoarsely, "I think she's dead."

Mia asked sharply, "Have you called an ambulance?"

"Oh yes, Ms. Mia," Dorrie panted. "The police were the ones who found her this time, thank God. I don't think I could handle finding another dead body." She made the sign of the cross. "She never rang for breakfast since she was still asleep. Or dead."

Dorrie went back to the hospitality team room to spread her news, and the three of them headed for Grand Palmettos Cottage.

The first person they saw was Sergeant Waters, grimly installing yellow crime scene tape around the cottage. Guests were gathered in small groups around the area, talking quietly and frowning. People did not look happy to be staying at a hotel with a probable murderer.

Mia sighed when she saw the bright yellow tape. "My kids are never going to let me live this down. Two murders while I'm staying here."

"Do you think it's another murder?" Rebecca asked with horror.

"I think the police are putting up crime scene tape around the cottage which means they think it might be a murder." She went up to Sergeant Waters and quietly asked, "Is Mrs. Winley dead?"

Sergeant Waters nodded brusquely and whispered, "Died in her sleep. Suspected homicide." In her official tones, she ordered, "Step back, please, ma'am."

Mia moved back and quickly texted her son, Mark, with the new event, then quickly turned her phone to silent to avoid his questions. "This is a PR nightmare."

"That poor girl," Rebecca gently chided her.

"I know," Mia agreed sadly. "A wasted life is incredibly sad. She was so young and stupid. Hannah Winley never really grew up, and now she'll never have a chance to."

7

Footprints in the Sand

ia headed straight for the main hotel. Her drunken rambling last night had made Hannah Winley into Mia's prime suspect. She wondered how easy it would have been for the murderer to slip something into her drink? The bar wasn't open this early in the day so she headed for Maria's office.

Maria was on the phone when she entered. "Yes, of course. If you'd like to reserve the ballroom at a later time," her voice dropped discretely, "when our recent trouble is cleared up, please let me know." She frowned, saying brightly, "Of course, I completely understand." She hung up and looked despondently at Mia, "That's the second major event cancelled today."

"It was inevitable."

"I know," Maria fiddled with her paperwork. "At least I think I have an alibi for this murder. I was at

Jake's baseball game, then we took him out for a celebration. We didn't get back until late."

Mia shook her head, "I think the murderer used poison. She died in her sleep."

"Well, shoot," Maria said with disgust. "I hoped at least Sam and I would have alibis. He should, anyway. Wasn't he at the police station all night?"

"He came home in the middle of the night," Mia informed her.

"Just gets better and better." She gestured in frustration at her stack of paperwork. "Not speaking from a personal viewpoint, this murder has to get solved soon or our busy season will be a bust."

"I know." Mia reassured her, "We will weather it. This is a temporary setback only."

"Yes," Maria agreed pugnaciously. "As soon as the murder's solved, we'll come right back." She smiled tightly, "I've already set up a security upgrade."

"Good." Mia got down to business, "So where was Hannah last night? I left her about eleven o'clock in the bar. She was drinking heavily." She thought a minute, "She said Trey was asking Sissy Collinsworth for money too. She pretty much drove Sissy out of the bar."

"Interesting," Maria sorted through files. "Here's the info on the Green Environmental Charity's fundraiser." She smiled grimly, "They haven't cancelled yet."

Mia started glancing through the fundraiser details. "Pretty elaborate affair," she commented.

"Yes, from what Sissy says they go all out. I think it still raises a fair amount for charity, though."

"That's nice," Mia said absently, looking through the numbers. "Have they ever held an event here before?"

"Not here, but she mentioned one of the other Spinel Hotels. Maybe Boston?" Maria offered.

"Mind if I borrow your desk for a few minutes? I think I'll make a few phone calls."

"No problem," Maria said. "I need to go take care of some things right now anyway." She bustled away.

Mia called the Spinel Boston's manager and after mutual greetings asked, "Do you remember a fundraiser for the Green Environmental Charity? Maybe run by a Sissy Collinsworth?"

The heartfelt sigh reverberated down the phone line, "Do I ever. That one was twice the work for half the profit. I swear that woman stayed at the hotel for a month before the event, going over every single solitary detail. And they got the charity discount for everything, even her stay." His voice sharpened, "Does this have anything to do with," he hesitated, "the little problem you're having on the Georgia coast?"

"It may," Mia told him. "Do you know of any other hotels that dealt with Sissy Collinsworth or the Green Environmental Charity?"

"Let's see, she mentioned some eco lodge in Patagonia, maybe another eco friendly one in the Amazon, that they'd been to. Little places." She heard a smile in his voice, "I think one of the major sponsors was in Boston and couldn't travel to the normal backwoods place, so they chose us as the most eco friendly in the area. I've noticed the quality of the hotels the charity events are at seems to have stepped up after they stayed here. Probably the older donors are tired of roughing it. I think the last was in one of the big Hawaiian resorts. And before that, the St. Johns in San Francisco. I'm not sure how many events they do a year."

"Interesting," Mia said. "Can you send me the paperwork from the event?"

"Will do," he said brightly. "We're looking forward to your next visit here, Mia. Just tell me when."

"Thanks, I am too," Mia said. The email came in a few minutes later. She studied it for a few minutes and did some online research. Then she called the St. Johns and asked to speak to the manager. A few minutes later, a familiar voice came over the line, "Mia? Is that really you, darling? It's John Blont, from Sydney."

"John? So that's where you ended up," Mia was glad to hear one of her old assistant managers on the line.

"It's all because of the name, darling. I couldn't resist."

"Why in the world would you? I was just talking about the fabulous St. Johns afternoon teas the other day."

"Oh yes, they're worth the trip. Next time you're in the area, we must have tea. I promise I'll pull out all the stops for my old boss."

"That sounds wonderful, John." Mia paused, "I have a problem with one of your former employees."

"So what's the problem?" he asked insouciantly.

"He was murdered yesterday at the hotel."

The phone went silent. "Oh." After a minute, he asked quietly, "Which hotel? And which employee?"

"Spinel Grand Island, on the Georgia coast, and Trey Sulley."

"Damn. Maria must be hopping mad."

"That she is." Mia went on grimly, "And a guest, Mrs. Hannah Winley, was murdered this morning."

"The Mrs. Arthur Winley?"

"Yes."

"Damn," he repeated.

"I hoped you might tell me a bit about Trey Sulley's history. He had only been here a little over a month and the St. Johns is his last employer."

"Off the record?" he asked cautiously.

"Of course, with me," Mia told him. "However I imagine the police will be contacting you as well."

"I see," he said hesitantly.

"I will mention, off the record, that Mr. Sulley seems to have blackmailed several guests..." Mia broke off.

"Ah. Yes, I see," John said. "Well, you're right, we weren't happy with Mr. Sulley here. His work was acceptable, but his demeanor was too casual for our clientele. I thought he would integrate better into a beach resort, as I told Maria when she called me." He assured her, "It was more about his comportment with guests than his actual work."

Mia read between the lines, "But you had other problems..."

"Not problems. Not problems, per se," John told her. "Anything definite and I'd have made sure Maria knew. But with all the employment regulations, you can't say anything except the facts in an experience letter unless you have proof in triplicate. And even then, they can sue you for defamation if you can't prove it in court." He sighed, "I keep them as short as possible for unsatisfactory employees."

"Was Trey unsatisfactory?" Mia persisted.

"He never did anything I could document besides the informal attitude toward guests." He sighed again, "I had several guests ask questions about him privately that seemed," he paused, "odd."

"What sort of questions?"

"Questions about his access to their rooms, their information. Could he open the room safe?" John's voice was disturbed. "I just got a very bad feeling about it. I had my security overhauled and about that time Trey informed me he was leaving."

"Interesting," Mia mused.

"I never had proof of anything. If I had, I would have told Maria privately," he assured her again.

Mia believed him, but she also knew he'd passed on a blackmailer to her hotel like a hot potato. She didn't blame him for getting rid of Trey, but she wasn't happy.

"Of course, I'll tell her that," Mia smoothly told him. "Well, it appears he continued his activities at my hotel."

"I'm sorry." John was clearly just glad to not have two murders at his hotel and a bit nervous of Maria's wrath, not to mention Mia's.

"I just need to ask you about one other thing that's come up."

"Anything at all," he told her fervently, glad she wasn't yelling at him and hoping to win back points.

"I have a Sissy Collinsworth staying here, planning a fundraiser for the Green Environmental Charity."

"Ah, dear Sissy," John said sourly. "She jabbered on about every single detail for ages. I think she managed to stay here two weeks, at the charity's expense, not ours, thank goodness. There wasn't a decision she couldn't stretch into a whole day."

"Did she have much contact with Mr. Sulley?"

"Well yes, she did, as a matter of fact," John mused. "He was events manager at that time, so she would have dealt primarily with him." He sardonically added, "She certainly managed to eat up a lot of my hours as well, though."

"Could you send me the paperwork on the event, if it's not too much trouble?" Mia requested. "I've noticed a few discrepancies in the numbers between their online records and the Spinel Boston's."

"Interesting," drew out John. "I would send you anything that made it possible she'd never come back to this hotel. Under the table, of course." He asked curiously, "Do you think she's the murderer?"

"I don't know," Mia said thoughtfully.

"You couldn't find a more abrasive one."

"Have you ever met Harold Stone, the writer?"

"Oh, you do have a full house there, darling." John laughed sarcastically. "Does he insist on drinking in the lobby?"

"Oh yes," Mia said with distaste. "Every day."

"Was Trey blackmailing him?"

"I don't know yet. I think maybe he was," Mia said. "Frankly, I suspected Mrs. Hannah Winley."

"And since she's dead, it's clearly not her." John said seriously, "She stays, I should say stayed, here fairly often with her husband, you know."

"Really? And did she do anything that she might be blackmailed for?"

"We pride ourself on our discretion." John said sardonically. "She did not do anything here I'd repeat. Mr. Sulley might have, however."

"I see."

"Whom else do you suspect? This is getting interesting."

"Since you seem to know everyone else, the police are erroneously suspecting an employee's husband, Sam Forrest."

"I don't know him."

"You wouldn't; he's an Atlanta lawyer. Nice man and his wife, Spinel's HR director, is amazing."

She continued, "Allison Jayton is from San Francisco, I think."

"Allison Jayton..." he mused. "Oh yes, she and her partner used to come to tea at the hotel every Friday for their weekend kickoff. So sad when her partner, Cindy Silvers, I think it was, died in that car crash. Beautiful girl, so quiet and sweet. Allison was the talker in that pair," he sighed. "She has the most gorgeous black hair, doesn't she? Really striking with those bright blue eyes and does she know how to dress."

"She still does, beautiful Paris fashions, straight off the runway," Mia told him, thinking furiously. Allison had told her she'd never been to the St. Johns. "Did they know Mr. Sulley?"

"They might have run across each other," he said. "They never planned any events for their company here, I know that. I think it was real estate or something. All online anyway. Quite a tragedy, all over the news. Allison never came to tea after that, either."

"I guess that was too painful a reminder." The St. Johns must be a heartrending memory for Allison. No wonder it was easier to say she hadn't been there.

"Yes," John agreed. "Who else?"

She continued, "Mr. and Mrs. Harry Browning have been questioned. They don't seem suspicious to me, but you never know. They're enthusiastic birdwatchers."

"That sounds familiar. Lots of birdwatchers stay here on their way to a more remote location. I'll check my books." She could hear him typing rapidly. "Right, they stayed here last fall for three days. That would have overlapped with Mr. Sulley's employment."

"So they're definitely on my suspect list still," Mia sighed. "It's not growing any shorter."

"I'll ask my staff about the Brownings and get back to you." He paused, "I'd say leave it to the police to clean up a murder, but I know you too well." John's tone sharpened, "I wouldn't leave it alone if it happened in my hotel either. I'll send you that file. Let me know if you need anything else."

"I will. Thanks, John."

As she hung up the phone, Captain Daniels came into the office, knocking on the open door. "Mrs. Sotos?" He did a double take, "Ms. Mia?"

"Yes, Danny?" She smiled at his confusion. "I'm just taking care of some business. Can I help you?"

"I was just letting Mrs. Sotos know we're done with Mrs. Winley's cottage."

"What happened to her?" Mia asked bluntly.

"We think someone slipped a lethal dose of barbiturates into her drink last night. She went to bed and never woke up."

"I was in the bar with her in the evening," Mia offered. "She was quite drunk at that point."

"Yes, the barkeeper told me you'd been questioning her," Danny informed her. "Did she say anything interesting?"

"I'm not sure. She was talking a lot about money. Hannah was drunk by the time I had a drink with her. She had an argument with her lawyers at dinner and threw a glass of water in one man's face."

"We heard about that," Danny said wryly.

"I assume her husband had found out about Phillip."

"Probably."

"She was crying about a prenuptial agreement and that she needed money."

Mia frowned, thinking through the alcoholic haze Hannah had spoken in. "She said she knew where she was going to get money."

"Interesting." Danny connected the dots, "So she decides to blackmail someone who's already killed their blackmailer? Brilliant."

"She was not the most intelligent woman," Mia said in a prim tone.

"I'll say."

"Sissy Collinsworth was also in the bar that night."

Danny looked up alertly, "Really."

"She was sitting behind us. Hannah pointed at Sissy and squawked on about Trey asking her for money too. Sissy left very abruptly after that."

"I see." Danny nodded. "I think I'll need that search warrant for Ms. Collinsworth's room after all." He frowned at her, "You can't come on an official search."

"Okay," Mia said agreeably. She had other fish to fry anyway.

8

Time Out

After a brief consultation with Sullivan, she found Sylvie on the beach, in the opposite direction from Hannah's cottage and where Trey's body was found.

She sat huddled in a limp heap in the dunes, crying her eyes out. When she saw Mia, Sylvie jumped up, startled, then collapsed again, too upset to care about anyone seeing her cry.

"Honey, what's wrong?" Mia sat down on the step next to her. "Can I help?"

"It's just a mess," the bedraggled woman cried. "I hate Harold. It's hell working with him. He screamed at me for an hour this morning then told me to get out."

Mia told her gently but firmly, "Sylvie, you can leave. Find another job where you're treated right. You have options."

"No, I don't!" she burst out. "I'm under contract to write three more books for him! I can't leave, or I'll never get to write again." She cried uncontrollably.

Mia realized with a start, "You wrote his last books? The best sellers?"

Sylvie wiped her face quickly, trying to regain control. "I'm not supposed to say. It's in the contract."

Mia nodded, "As soon as I saw him at the hotel, I was surprised he'd written those books." She smiled, "I enjoyed his last few books, but the ones before that weren't likable at all. You, my dear, are a much better writer."

The woman panicked, "I can't say anything about it. I'd lose everything and never get to write again. I don't have anything else I know how to do."

"No, no, you haven't said a thing," Mia reassured her. "I certainly don't remember anything."

"Thanks," Sylvie sighed, grateful tears forming. "It just got to be too much, dealing with Harold. And the murders. He's terrified they'll think it's him so he's taking it out on me."

"I can believe that," Mia said with feeling. She looked at the tear streaked woman, her lank hair hanging limply in clumps. "He's a jerk," she said bluntly.

"Yeah, I wish I'd known before I started working for him." Sylvie's voice was bitter, "I was just too excited to work with the great Harold Stone. I signed on the dotted line before I knew what I was doing. Stupid."

Mia smiled at her, "We're all stupid at least once." She patted Sylvie's shoulder, "Let's think of how to get you out of this. We'll start with washing your face and a good brisk walk."

Mia stood up, pulling Sylvie with her. "That will get you started on a better track." She hurried the woman into the beach bathhouse, so she'd look presentable, then started walking her down the beach. She was going to straighten out this mess Sylvie had gotten herself into. And she knew a way to investigate the murders at the same time.

Sylvie looked a little more positive as they walked along the beach. Mia kept her to a brisk walk, not letting Sylvie slow to her normal dragging pace. "You need a day off to start. Text Harold and say you're sick."

"I think I can do that," Sylvie said hesitatingly. "He'll probably just drink in his room all day."

"Good. He won't disturb the lobby all afternoon then," Mia said decisively. "We're going to the spa. He won't go there."

"Oh, I couldn't," Sylvie demurred. "It would show up on the hotel bill. He complains if I get room service even."

"Don't worry, I'll take care of it."

Sylvie still looked reluctant.

"You can dedicate your first book with your own name on it to me," Mia grinned with anticipation. "I can't wait to see what you can do unfettered."

She kept walking, her sandals slapping emphatically on the sidewalk. Sylvie paused, then hurried to catch up. "Do you really think I could?"

"Oh yes," Mia said with confidence. "You absolutely will." She went on with her plan. "We'll go to the spa.

It's amazing how much better you'll feel with a little time out for yourself. I know I always do."

"Next, I know a great lawyer staying here. He's on vacation, but you can meet him now and give him your contract to look over. If I know Sam, he'll consider it a fun challenge." She nodded with decision, "If anyone can get you out of this mess, Sam Forrest can." It would make Sam feel less helpless in his own mess too.

"Really?" Sylvie started to look hopeful after being cocooned in her own misery for so long. "Do you really think?"

"Oh yes," Mia said. "And trust me, the resort team will back you up on how badly he treats you. You don't just have to take it."

They went straight to the long low spa building. Mia was not giving Sylvie a chance to back out. A koi pond with a soft waterfall splashed in the foyer, creating a sense of calm peace. They felt their spirits lift.

The round faced receptionist greeted them cheerfully, "Ms. Mia! I was wondering when you'd stop by."

"It's good to see you, Misty. I brought my friend Sylvie. I hoped you could fit us in."

"Of course, Ms. Mia," she said enthusiastically, her bright blue eyes shining and sleek ponytail dancing. "What would you like? The works?"

"Absolutely, Misty," Mia said happily. "That sounds perfect. Do you have some hair appointments as well today? I've just had mine done in London, but I think my friend here would like some work."

"Oh, but..." Sylvie began but Mia shushed her.

"No problem, Mr. Henry is free at two." Misty typed in the schedule.

"Perfect, then we'll have a light lunch next to the pool and have ourselves a spa day." She smiled in happy anticipation at Sylvie. "This is going to be so nice." She thought of something, "You know, why don't I ask Allison to join us? Girls day at the spa sounds perfect."

At Sylvie's nod, she invited Allison, who sounded pleased at being asked. Mia had a quiet word with Misty, planning their day. When Allison arrived, Mia swept them into the spa.

"It's been a long time since I have done anything like this," Sylvie told her, giggling a bit.

Mia smiled at her, "You just have to take time for yourself, no matter what."

"Absolutely," Allison assured Sylvie. She seemed very proud of being included in the spontaneous fun with one of the hotel owners.

Misty smiled and shepherded them to treatment rooms, "Why don't you begin with a nice massage, then skin treatments?"

Mia relaxed into bliss at her massage, feeling the remnants of jet lag melt away under her masseur's deft touch. She could hear muffled sounds of Sylvie squealing in pain at her massage. The poor girl was so tense—she needed to relax.

However, Mia had picked her particular masseuse for a reason. "Jasmine, that feels wonderful."

The tiny woman said cheerfully as she pummeled her back, "It's good to see you back, Ms. Mia. I was wondering when you'd get here."

"I got distracted by the murders," Mia told her.

Her attack slowed a minute, "I know, it's just awful, isn't it? Mrs. Winley was here most of the day yesterday."

"That's right," Mia said silkily. "I sent her here to get over the shock of Mr. Sulley's death."

"Yeah, she was pretty upset. Her muscles were so tense she yelped every time I touched her, just about." She could hear Jasmine stop smiling when she remembered. "Can't believe she's dead."

"I know. It's terrible," Mia agreed. She paused a moment then asked, "Did she say anything that might give a hint of why she was killed yesterday?"

"I've been thinking," Jasmine said. "We chatted, like we usually do, you know? Some people like to talk while they're getting a massage; some people don't, like the other lady you brought with you today. Allison likes her quiet time, which is fine by me. Hannah would talk a mile a minute, all about herself."

"What sort of things?"

"Well, she was pretty picky about her massage. Seemed to think a massage would make up for all the drinking she did. I think it pretty likely she did a bit more than drinking, too." Jasmine gave a knowing sniff. "That sort of thing takes a pretty hefty toll on your body. She was terrified of losing her looks."

"Was she?" Mia was curious.

"Most likely," Jasmine said with a shrug. "She needed a bit more help here than last year. A bit more makeup to look perfect. I think she'd had some botox since last time too."

"So young for all that."

174

"Well, I think she was a bit older than she looked. Nearer thirty than twenty, for sure. She was aging fast, even with all the care she took." Jasmine moved to deep tissue massage her legs. Mia felt tiny knots melt as she worked.

Jasmine continued, "She tied her looks to money, in a big way. She didn't want to end up back where she'd started in Kansas again. She liked her men—that Phillip guy was handsome, like a movie star, wasn't he? But she liked her money more. She was talking about someone who'd pay her lots of money."

"Didn't her husband give her plenty of money? She certainly seemed to spend a lot," Mia thought of the expensive clothes and jewelry strewn about Hannah's cottage.

"Did you hear about that scene with his lawyers last night?" At Mia's nod, she went on, "I think she saw the writing on the wall with her marriage. She'd signed a prenup and would get hardly anything when the marriage was over." Jasmine shook her head with disapproval, "She had the morals of an alley cat and that wouldn't be hard to prove."

"No," Mia said thoughtfully. "Do you have any idea who she was going to get money from?"

"Someone she'd known before, from a long time ago." Jasmine sighed, "I figure she knew who Trey's murderer was and kept it to herself for blackmail. Such a stupid waste."

"I know. So very young," Mia sighed. "I wonder if she saw the murder?"

"She might have, at that," Jasmine thought aloud. "She was really upset when she came in yesterday. Worried about money and her looks, but almost crying too. Really upset. It'd make sense if she'd seen the murder."

"Poor girl," Mia said. It was a fitting epitaph for Hannah Winley, the poor little rich girl.

They emerged from the massages and were ushered into the main treatment room. Sylvie looked like she'd been wrung out like a dishrag. Her masseuse fussed around her, telling her she must come back within the week, without fail. Sylvie blindly agreed.

Mia smiled. She thought Sylvie would agree to anything right now. It was a good thing she was in charge.

The spa walls enveloped them in lovely pink marble with delicate swirls of white, lit with flattering light. Glass doors opened onto a tropical green courtyard at the far end, making the large room seem like a secret grotto. Soft piano music merged with a waterfall's splashes at the far end. Cream colored treatment couches were set up grouped around a long pool so friends could get facials together with some private rooms for solitary guests, like movie stars recouping from treatments far from the public eye.

A few of the wedding guests still here had chosen to relax, away from the outside world. She overheard one of the mothers saying to the other, "When he brought her home, I just knew we'd have a wedding."

The other mother nodded in happy agreement and Mia smiled. That was the wonderful part about weddings and hotels. They brought people together to have fun.

She relaxed in her soft cotton robe, sinking into the couch and smiled over at Sylvie, "Feeling better?"

"I can't remember last time I had a massage. I really needed it," Sylvie said, grimacing a little.

"Get another in about three days," Mia advised. "That will get rid of the soreness."

The aesthetician came over and smiled at them. She had fresh clear skin that showed off her art and medium brown hair confined by a smooth headband. "Ms. Mia, so good to see you!"

"Hi, Elizabeth, good to see you too."

"What would you girls like today?"

"I'd like just a little help getting over jet lag, but my friend here wants the works."

"Hmm," Elizabeth frowned as she examined Sylvie's pinched face. Sylvie squirmed under her professional gaze.

"You have lovely skin, but it looks like you've been under a lot of stress lately," her verdict was. "I know the perfect masque to help your skin, then some smoothing treatments. I have the most wonderful pomegranate oil you will absolutely love." She smiled reassuringly, "It won't take long at all for your skin to be beautiful again."

She turned to Mia, "I'll get started with Sylvie here, then you'd like your usual, Ms. Mia? And you, Ms. Jayton?"

"I've been outside so much the past few days." Allison thought a minute, "How about a soothing facial, with an antioxidant treatment? Would that work for me?"

"Of course, Ms. Jayton," Elizabeth told her. "That should be perfect for your skin today."

Mia relaxed in the soft pink world of the spa, enjoying being cared for so beautifully. Her facial soothed her with the delicate scent of magnolia and gardenia. She loved the water reflections shimmering on the ceiling and the soft splash of the waterfall.

After the treatments, they enjoyed a quiet little lunch beside the long pool, where spa goers continued to relax in their soft white robes, free from the rest of the world.

Sylvie seemed overwhelmed by the entire experience, quietly taking in the spa room from behind her big glasses.

"Feeling relaxed?" Mia asked.

"Oh yes," Sylvie said luxuriating in her surroundings. She slowly savored a bite of fish in a miso ginger sauce.

Mia smiled and let her enjoy the experience. "I know you've visited the spa before, Allison. What's your favorite treatment?"

"I'm not sure," Allison said. "I love the hot stone massage best, I think. So relaxing. The sound of the waterfall and pool just make it all feel like a lovely dream. Reminds me of hiking in Costa Rica."

"I'm so glad. Have you been hiking there often?"

"No, just twice. Wonderful trips. I only started being able to afford to go to spas and travel a few years ago. And I never took off much time to do things like this before I sold my company." Allison smiled sadly, "It seems so awful to be enjoying all this without my partner."

"You were close?" Mia asked sympathetically.

"Very," Allison looked back in time what seemed like a long way. "We both moved to Los Angeles at about the same time, wanted to be movie stars." She laughed, "Cindy and I proved to be much better at selling real estate than finding acting jobs. We moved to San Francisco, went online, and the rest was history." She smiled sadly, "Cindy would have loved this place."

"Then let's drink to Cindy," Mia said, lifting her glass.

They chorused, "To Cindy." Allison discretely wiped a tear away.

"I think I'll go sailing this afternoon," she said, changing the subject.

"That sounds like fun. The bay here is made for little sailboats."

After lunch, Misty arrived to shepherd Sylvie to Mr. Henry's domain. Mia went along to make sure Sylvie didn't run from Henry's suggestions. He could be a little overwhelming.

The tall, thin man walked around Sylvie, making little tsking noises, "My dear, you have not been taking care of your hair. It could be gorgeous, but you need to tend it." He shook his head at her neglect, pulling strands away with his long clever fingers and dropping them limply. "You need to take care of yourself better."

"I know, I know," Sylvie shrunk a little in the chair, looking scared.

"Oh, don't worry, dear Sylvie. We'll have it looking gorgeous in no time." He frowned at her hair, planning the cut.

"Definitely with an easy to maintain style, Henry. She's a busy woman," Mia cut in.

"Oh, don't worry, Ms. Mia. I'll have it where it's easy to take care of. I don't think she'll even need color, just a little brightening up." He held up a hunk of the lank blonde hair. "Let's start with a wash and treatment." He grandly motioned to one of his underlings, and she led the nervous Sylvie to one of the sink cubicles.

"You're here for a few weeks, Ms. Mia?" the hair stylist asked, relaxing from his impressive public persona. "I do want to give you a tiny bit of shaping before you leave, but I wouldn't want to take any off now."

"Yes, I had mine done at the London hotel. He did a very nice job, but I do prefer your touch," Mia agreed. "I'll come in for a refresh in a week or two."

He looked up as Sylvie came in, looking like a wrung dishrag. "Ah, Sylvie, my dear! Are you ready to be beautiful?" he enthused.

Sylvie looked nervously at Mia and she nodded, "Just put yourself in his hands, honey. You'll be gorgeous."

And she was. Two hours later, Sylvie looked at herself in the mirror and smiled shyly. "Is that really me?"

"It's all you, sweetie," Henry told her. "Just shaped up a bit." He beamed in pride.

Mia smiled, "You look beautiful."

"I do, don't I?" Her glossy hair was shaped into a long bob, complimenting her face perfectly. Her skin radiated health. Sylvie looked relaxed and happy. "This is me," she told herself in the mirror.

"Perfect. Thanks, Henry." Mia stood up, stretching. She'd had a manicure and a nice glass of bubbly while she waited, but she was ready to get moving again. The spa was obviously running beautifully, and she didn't need to worry about it, just enjoy it over the next few weeks.

Sylvie came out, swinging her hair softly in enjoyment. "I love it. I wish I'd done that ages ago. Thank you so much for making me do it."

"It's never too late to do anything," Mia said firmly. "Now, I need to check out a few things before dinner. You relax, dress for dinner and I'll meet you at 8:00. The resort team will send you to whichever dining room Harold isn't in, and I'll meet you there."

"Thank you, Mia," Sylvie said. "I feel like everything is possible again."

"Of course it is," Mia told her. "Sometimes you just need a time out and restart."

Instead of going directly back to her room, Mia went to the main hotel and knocked on Sam and Rebecca's room. Sam opened the door cautiously on the chain, then quickly let Mia in. Rebecca came in from the balcony, where she had been sitting.

"How are you?"

"Hanging in there," Rebecca said wryly. Her usual intense vitality was gone, and it made Mia sad just to see her downcast face.

"We've stayed in the room most of the day. Unfortunately Mrs. Winley's death did not give me an alibi. It made me less likely, but still a firm suspect, according to Captain Daniels." Sam sat in the armchair, feet propped up casually but tense as a harp string. "I'm very lucky he's holding off arresting me with the evidence he has."

"I thought you didn't come back until very late from the police station?"

"Yes, but there's no way to tell to the hour when Mrs. Winley received the opiate that killed her. Or how," Sam told her. "They found a bottle of expensive Scotch in her cottage they think contained the drug. I haven't drunk Scotch this trip, so my fingerprints could not possibly be on it." He let out a deep breath. "Of course, I don't imagine whoever put it there left their fingerprints on it."

"No, I wouldn't think so." Mia thought a minute. "Hannah came to the bar to drink because she was out of alcohol in her room. I'm not sure why she didn't call for room service, but she walked over instead."

"Probably wanted some company, poor girl," Rebecca said softly.

"Probably," Mia agreed. "So all someone would have to do would be to leave a bottle of Scotch on her doorstep. She'd give herself a nightcap when she tucked in for the night. They wouldn't even have to go in the door."

"Anyone could do it," Sam stated. "And I went and walked on the beach for a minute when I got back to the hotel. I needed to clear my head." He hung his head a minute, "I was probably right next to her cottage near the time the murderer left his little present."

182

"I wish you'd come straight back," Rebecca said dismally, brown eyes red rimmed.

"Did you see anyone?" Mia asked, practically.

"I've been racking my head on that. I vaguely remember a few people, even at that time of night. I wasn't really in a state to concentrate on random people."

He said slowly, "That batty woman who walks in the surf was wandering around, raising her hands to mother moon or something. I remember her because she made me decide to go the other direction." He smiled ruefully, "I was not in the mood for moon worshipers."

"She was really worshiping the moon?" Rebecca asked curiously.

"It certainly looked like it," Sam said with disgust. "Around where the body was found. She was standing in the surf, long skirt floating around and hands up towards the moon over the water, chanting something." He made a face. "I didn't get close enough to hear what she was saying. Just did a rightabout and walked the other way."

"I don't blame you. I do the same thing when I see her," Mia said ruefully. "Did you notice anyone else?"

He closed his eyes, his long face weary behind his glasses. He ran a hand over his smoothly cropped hair. "I think I saw someone or more moving on the dunes near that woman. I remember vaguely thinking that I hoped a cult wasn't starting on the island."

"In the dunes? So possibly on the side path next to Hannah's cottage?"

Sam nodded, eyes still closed to aid memory. "Just a shadow in the dark." He shook his head, "Yes, there was definitely something at the edge of the palmettos." He looked at her, "It could have been deer, but something was there." He concentrated harder. "When I got back to the terrace, I saw that birdwatching couple. They had night vision goggles and other gear all over them and were coming inside."

"Probably looking at owls again," Mia said.

Rebecca put in, "Yeah, but birdwatching would be a really good excuse to be anywhere on the grounds at unexpected times."

"It would indeed." Mia looked at Sam's opened eyes. "Anyone else?"

"I'm sorry, I just can't think of anyone else. It was just dark, with the wind blowing from the sea. Enough moonlight to see people, but that was it." He exhaled heavily, "I wish I had noticed."

"I wish you had too." Mia looked at Sam, "I have a project for you." She handed him a dollar bill. "This is your retainer for listening to Sylvie Summers' case."

"Okay," Sam scribbled a note, signed it and got Mia to do the same. "What's going on?"

"She's the one writing Harold Stone's books." They stared at her. "The last three bestsellers? Hers."

"Wow, that explains a lot," Rebecca exclaimed. "I wondered how he could write like that when he can't even speak coherently."

"Exactly."

"So she's in a contract?" Sam asked professionally.

"And I want you to get her out of it," Mia stated. "You've seen how he treats her."

"He'll take the case," Rebecca told him firmly.

He looked at her and Mia. It was clearly two against one with only one way out. "Okay, okay. I'll read the contract and we'll go from there." He smiled at them, "I enjoyed those books too. It will be a pleasure."

"Good." Mia stood up, "Okay, you two. Get ready to go on a boat ride."

They looked at her, confused. "Why?" asked Rebecca.

"Because you've sat brooding in this room long enough. I know you don't want to go out and have people bothering you," Mia told them. "You're both too tired to handle a boat by yourselves at night. So I've arranged with Billy to take you on a moonlight dinner cruise. He's taking the opportunity to take his grandson fishing. You get your dinner boat party and he gets his fishing trip."

They hesitated, not sure whether to leave the room.

"You wouldn't want to let a seven year old kid not have a fishing trip with his grandfather, would you?" Mia said craftily. "You can't possibly let him down."

Rebecca laughed, an echo of her old joy. "All right, you win, Mia."

"I'm going to walk you there," she told them.

"To make sure we go?" Sam asked.

"Possibly," Mia agreed. She waited while they changed into clothes for a boat ride. They came out quickly, traces of enthusiasm for their outing starting to show. Rebecca looked lovely in a cherry red jacket.

They collected two tremendous picnic baskets brimming with interestingly wrapped treats from the kitchens. Francisco, back at work, told them, "This is for you and this one for Billy and his grandson. I don't think

Billy wants to get his grandson hooked on champagne and caviar quite yet. Just to hook a fish."

He smiled at Mia, "I'm manning the Hammock restaurant tonight. If you come, I'll have something very special just for you."

"An omelette?" Mia teased.

"Not tonight," he told her, brown eyes laughing. "Have fun, you guys."

They thanked him and walked to the dock, where one of the hotel's Fountain 52 fishing boats waited for them. Billy, with a slew of fishing rods, was organizing his trip and grandson.

"Good, you've brought the food," he greeted them, his face creasing into an intricate network of wrinkles. "I think we're ready if you are."

"Absolutely," Rebecca enthused. Impulsively, she hugged Mia, "Thanks, Mia."

Sam nodded, eyes scanning the ultimate fishing boat with pure happiness.

"Anytime," Mia waved them into the harbor. She stood for a minute, looking out to sea. The dock was beautifully situated, just sheltered enough to protect boats from most storms, with a boathouse for smaller crafts and a fishing dock over on the side, with hoses and trays for cleaning the catch.

Quite a few guests brought their own boats. The island was a popular resort in the South for husbands to fish and golf, while their wives enjoyed the spa and beach as consolation prizes. Everyone was happy on their vacation, and they could meet up for dinner at the end of the day.

Mia wandered into the boat house. The boy behind the desk said, "Hello, Mrs. Spinel. Ready to take out a boat?"

"Not today," she looked for his name tag, "Josh. I'm just looking around."

"Yes, ma'am." He went back to his paperwork.

There were a few last minute things for sale, like cold drinks, fishing bait and other little extras people might have forgotten, but much of the boathouse contained loaner life jackets for the hotel boats and other gear they might need. Paddles for kayaks, lines and sails for small sailboats, oars for rowboats. The boats themselves were lined up around the central slip or in racks on the sides. Since part of the fun of staying on an island was the boats, they had a wide selection of anything a guest might enjoy.

Mia paused beside a small two person JY 15 sailboat. "That looks like fun."

"Oh yes, ma'am. Easy to single hand too. A lady has one out solo right now, as a matter of fact. Nice little boats. We've got a fleet of ten of them for races in the summer—the kids love them. Would you like to take one out?"

"Maybe in a few days," Mia considered. It had been a while since she sailed. "I'm a little busy right now."

"Yes, ma'am," the boy repeated, his Adam's apple bobbing. "I've been pretty busy today too," he volunteered.

"Lots of boaters out?"

"A fair amount," he grinned. "I guess Mrs. Sotos gave out boat discounts like crazy to keep guests here with the murders and stuff. I had to get one of the landscape guys to help, I was so busy."

Mia smiled, "I'm sorry about that, but you helped save the hotel from some heavy losses."

"Yes, ma'am." The Adam's apple bobbed again. "But it wasn't just that, you know. Someone broke into the boat house two nights ago and trashed it."

"Really?" Mia asked, surprised. "What did they do?"

"I figure it was kids, you know?" He waved a skinny arm vaguely. "They couldn't get a boat out—the door's too small and we lock the big door down, of course." He waved his arm again, "I mean, I have to check all the boats in, know where everyone is so we don't lose guests."

"Yes, of course."

"So they crawled in that window there," he swallowed hard in thought. "We leave it cracked at the top for air circulation, you know?"

She nodded.

"They crawled in there. Couldn't get a boat, so they went through everything. Moved stuff around everywhere. Life jackets all mixed up on a pile on the floor. Strung sailboat lines around like a spider's web." He gestured at the deep water in the middle. "I had to dive for some of it. I think I have one more dive left tomorrow, and I'll have it all."

He continued, still angry now at the extra work, "So I had to clean everything up, put it back where it was supposed to be. Untangling the lines took forever. I just finished doing inventory." He gestured at his open notebook.

"Was anything missing?"

"Nah, nothing valuable's missing, just moved around and messed with. That's why I figure it was kids trying to take a boat out. They just wanted a midnight sail, not to actually steal stuff."

"That makes sense," Mia agreed. "I'm sorry you had so much extra work on top of dealing with that."

"Nah, it's okay," he swallowed hard and waved his hands around, searching for words. "I mean, sometimes I just sit and study; sometimes it's crazy. You never know what the day's going to be."

"I hope you didn't have a test this week, then," Mia said sympathetically.

"Nah, not until next Friday. Mechanical engineering," he told her with pride. "I'm going to build boats someday."

"Good," Mia said with approval. "I'll send someone to put some bars on the window so you don't have to clean up like that again. We were lucky the break in caused so little damage, but there's no point in taking time away from your books when you don't have to."

"No, ma'am," he said with a grin. "Thanks."

She paused a moment to enjoy the sunset as she left the dock. The bright greens of the salt marshes were dulled and tinged with the red gold sky, decorated in swaths of red and purple. Huge cumulous clouds billowed on the horizon, almost hiding the sun. A golden ray emerged from behind a cloud, highlighting a distant patch of ocean. "Beautiful," she murmured to herself. "Just beautiful."

The sound of the waves gently slapping the dock and the smell of the sea calmed her. She saw gulls rising in the distant streaming light, lit like angels rising to above, their white feathers gleaming. Only their screams gave them away. Gulls were far from angels.

And so were humans.

She had been running around, these last few days, trying to solve the murders. She was mad at Trey's murderer, but almost angrier at Trey himself for blackmailing her guests and causing his own murder. In her hotel!

If he was still alive, she'd have taken great pleasure in firing him again and been much less nice about it.

The problem with blackmailers is they caused their own deaths by preying off the weak. When one of their prey fought back, well—it was the only obvious outcome.

Mia didn't doubt that Hannah had caused her own death the same way. Greedy and stupid was a combination always leading to an ultimate failure.

She now knew who had killed them both. She thought she knew the motive and the means. She just had to prove it.

Mia smiled and with her mind at peace, went back to her cottage to dress for dinner.

9

An Unexpected Treat

Mia dressed in bright turquoise blue, with a sparkling blue spinel bracelet and earrings to match. She slipped on some elegant high heeled sandals, draped a warm cashmere scarf around her neck, added a dash of bright pink lipstick and went to dinner.

Sullivan greeted her as she came in, "Hello, Ms. Mia. Your guest, Ms. Sylvie Summers, has already arrived. I've seated her in the Hammock Dining Room." He added discretely, "Mr. Harold Stone is in the Grand Palmettos Dining Room."

"Thank you, Sullivan."

"Ms. Summers looks like a different woman after her trip to the spa." He enthused, "Mr. Henry works miracles, doesn't he?"

"He really is the best," Mia agreed. "I'm glad he likes being here. We have quite a few guests that visit just for his transformations."

"All you have to do is look at Ms. Summers to see why." Sullivan smiled. "Will Ms. Jayton be joining you tonight?"

"I don't think so," Mia told him. "She mentioned something about sailing this afternoon. She'll probably be ready to relax in her room afterwards."

"Yes, that girl knows how to treat herself," Sullivan said. "I'm glad you kidnapped Ms. Summers though."

"Sometimes we need friends to force us to take a break."

The Hammock Dining Room was lovely tonight, with glossy leaved potted palm trees screening intimate white covered tables and pale turquoise walls. The headwaiter, Harrison, ushered her to the table where Sylvie waited.

Mia smiled when she saw Sylvie's new glow. She was obviously happier and feeling more like the person she should be.

Francisco came out to greet her, "I'm so glad you came, Ms. Mia. I have some treats for you and your guest tonight." He looked both nervous and excited at the menu he had chosen.

"Wonderful!" Mia smiled at him, "Please surprise us then." She told Sylvie, "I can't wait to find out."

A few minutes later, Francisco came out himself, bearing the appetizers. "I thought you might miss your days in Mexico, ma'am. Tonight, I've made you my favorite dishes my mother and grandmother taught me when I was growing up."

"How wonderful!" Mia looked forward to the treat.

"First, ceviche chile tamulado made with fish I caught myself this afternoon." He nervously flourished two small plates, with elegant fish arranged among fresh herbs.

"Lovely and delicious," Mia savored a bite of tangy ceviche. "Thank you, Francisco."

He departed, beaming.

"This is so good," Sylvie said. "What is that flavor? I don't think I've tasted anything like it before."

"It's a Seville orange and habanero combination. It brings me back to Mexico and fish dinners on the beach." Mia sighed in pleasure.

Harrison poured champagne for them. "May I say how beautiful your new hair style is, ma'am," he told Sylvie. "You look very glamorous tonight."

Sylvie giggled a little, blushing. "Thanks."

"It really looks lovely, Sylvie. Mr. Henry does amazing transformations, but it's all you," Mia agreed.

Harrison left, smiling in encouraging admiration.

"Speaking of transformations, I've retained Sam Forrest on your behalf. He's going to look over your contract and tell you what your best options are." She reassured Sylvie, "If anyone can get you out of it, Sam can."

Sylvie said uncertainly, "But surely he has his own troubles right now? I know the police questioned him about the murder."

"Oh, honey," Mia smiled. "Sam didn't commit any murders, and this will take his mind off his troubles while the murders are being solved."

"You think the police are that close to finding the murderer?"

"I think Captain Daniels is a very efficient officer," Mia told her mendaciously. She'd eat her hat if she didn't solve the case before Danny.

"So who do you think did it?" Sylvie asked.

"You know, I wonder if Harold Stone had a motive," Mia mused.

"Harold? Oh, I don't think so," Sylvie said with surprise.

"He had a motive," Mia nodded at Sylvie. "I don't know if he had opportunity," she wondered. "And he certainly could have used one of the steak knives from dinner. We keep them very sharp."

"Oh..." Sylvie went still for a moment. "His laptop went missing."

"Yes," Mia encouraged.

"Someone told me Trey was a blackmailer."

"He absolutely was," Mia confirmed.

Sylvie looked around her cautiously, then whispered, "So you think Harold was blackmailed about my ghostwriting his books?"

"It would definitely be a motive."

"He could prove it with information off the laptop, for sure," Sylvie said, warming to the theory. Then she suddenly frowned, "But how could he get to the beach at night? Wouldn't his key card show him leaving the room?"

Mia told her, "He was on the beach that night."

"Really?" Sylvie was clearly astounded. "He was actually on the beach." She frowned, concentrating.

"He said he didn't remember anything, but he was photographed on the beach close to the time Trey died. With a bottle," Mia added.

"He would be," said Sylvie, clearly nauseated. "I don't know if he'd murder anyone. He's got a temper, but I don't know if he has enough, well, drive, to murder someone." She looked uncomfortable. "When he says he doesn't remember, I'm sure he doesn't. He's been having trouble with blackouts. There are entire days he just forgets." She explained, "That's why he's terrified the police will think he's the murderer. And if he was actually on the beach that night..."

"So he's having alcoholic blackouts?"

"Look, he doesn't want anyone to know—it would kill his book sales."

"I doubt that," Mia said tartly.

"Yes, but," Sylvie leaned forward, obviously upset. "I hate the man, but I can't go blabbing to everyone about blackouts and murder. When it comes down to it, I have no idea if he'd even want to kill Trey."

"I don't either," Mia said. "He was mad at Trey, but murdering him is an entirely different story. And I don't know where he was last night yet. If Hannah saw Trey's murder, that would be a motive for her death."

Harrison presented their next course of an elevated pork tamale, tasting of achiote and smoke, surrounded by roasted peppers on a bed of chaya leaves. Beside the main course were polkanes, fried masa and pumpkin, in a hearty tomato onion sauce. Their talk turned to the food instead of the murder, giving the feast the full attention it deserved.

After the main course, Francisco served them pulpo en escabeche with an anxious flourish. "I hope you like octopus."

"I haven't had this in ages," Mia said with delight. "It's cooked, then marinated in an acid overnight," she told Sophie, tasting it. "Lime with a hint of sour orange." Tiny cubes of zucchini soaked in the sauce.

For the cheese course, Francisco tendered a queso relleno, a hollowed Edam cheese stuffed with barbecued pork and tomatoes and chiles.

They enjoyed their desserts of tiny delicate pastries containing chocolate piquantly spiced with chile and Seville oranges, savoring every bite.

After Francisco's wonderful feast, Mia went outside to the terrace, leaning on the cool stone of the balusters. She stood and looked out at the deep blue of the sky merging into the sea. Palmettos clattered overhead.

She went down to the beach, but somehow, walking away from the lighted beach into the dark wasn't particularly appealing tonight. The welcoming lights of the terrace felt like a smarter choice, with a murderer around. She shivered in her thin dress, wrapped her warm scarf tightly around her and went back to the terrace.

A few couples enjoyed nightcaps on the terrace, sipping their drinks and enjoying the ocean breeze.

People were winding down for the night, savoring their prelude to bed.

The Brownings perched at a prime spot on the terrace, scanning the native wildlife, both human and otherwise. Upon sighting her, Mrs. Browning called out, "Mrs. Spinel, please do come join us."

As Mia sat down with a smile, Mr. Browning enthused, "The trip to Bar Island was absolutely fantastic! We added ten more birds to our life lists, including whimbrels. Did you know they migrate all the way from Brazil to Nova Scotia every year? And the Sea Islands are a regular stop."

"In just one trip?" Mia had been around enough birders to know how big a deal this was. "That's wonderful!"

"We looked through our photos before dinner. You would not believe the diversity of birds on that one barrier island."

"Honestly, I'm always surprised at the diversity of birds I see here during spring and fall migrations. I see birds I've never seen before all the time." Mia smiled at their avid faces. "I'm not a birder, unfortunately, but the wildlife has always been one of my favorite things about the island."

"Oh, but you should keep track of what you see here," Mr. Browning said, slightly obsessively. "It's so helpful to know where you've seen a certain species of bird before."

"I'm sure you're right," Mia demurred. Really, she just liked looking at birds. She didn't feel like keeping track of them. Birds could do that all by themselves.

"There should be some sort of wildlife center on the island," Mrs. Browning suggested. "We've found some birds on the island that weren't in local guides. Not even the Colonial Coast Birding Trail guide. Grand Island is really an ecological treasure."

"I've always felt so. We feel very strongly about preserving the pristine areas of the island." Mia thought a minute, "You know, that's a terrific idea. My manager has been looking for ideas to keep older kids busy on rainy days. If we combined that with a nature center, they could have fun and maybe learn a little."

"It makes such a difference for kids to learn about wildlife early," Mrs. Browning said ardently.

Mia was still thinking, "We have nature hikes and talks already. One place to organize lectures and small events would be perfect." She smiled enthusiastically at them, "I'll talk to my manager about it. Thanks for the idea."

"It's a good idea," Mrs. Browning agreed eagerly. She was just tipsy enough to agree to almost anything now. "And it will give her something to concentrate on besides those horrible murders."

"I know," Mia said with a sigh. "I wish they hadn't happened here."

"Oh well, Hannah was just asking for trouble one way or another," Mrs. Browning said with a moue of distaste. "I know Art's had his hands full with that one."

"Now, Susan," Mr. Browning said. "No one deserves that."

"Well, of course not, Harry. But she was very indiscrete with her affairs."

"That's her husband's business, Susan. Not ours."

Mrs. Browning's tongue was slightly loosened by her nightcap. "Harry, she was just asking for trouble. Why, we saw her wandering around at night off the dunes. One affair was just not enough for her. A woman like that is headed for trouble."

"When did you see her?" Mia asked curiously.

"At night. She'd just lie on the beach all day. I don't think I saw her walking on the trails even once."

"I mean, what night did you see her?"

Mr. Browning thought back, "We went owling a few nights ago. Is that what you meant?"

"Yes, it was three, no, two nights ago. The night we saw the great horned owl pair." Mrs. Browning was looking fairly owlish herself.

"Was it the night of Trey Sulley's murder?" Mia pressed her.

Mrs. Browning stared at her with big, slightly unfocused eyes. "Was that the night of the murder?" She looked at her husband for confirmation.

"I think it must have been," he agreed uncomfortably. "It was definitely the night we saw the great horned owls." He got his phone out, looking at his calendar.

"Oh dear, I didn't tell the police," Mrs. Browning said, upset.

"Don't worry, just tell them in the morning. They'll understand a lot was happening," Mia assured her. "What was she doing?"

"She was wandering on the dunes," Mr. Browning told her. "We walked on the beach, then cut over the dunes on the boardwalks. She was off the boardwalk, walking around."

"Sneaking. And destroying the dunes," Mrs. Browning cut in.

"Now dear," Mr. Browning soothed. "There were other people out that night as well. We saw that nice young lawyer taking a walk. He took a walk on the beach late last night too. We saw him returning."

His wife nodded approvingly. "I've seen him running in the morning, not just lazing around like Hannah." She remembered, "I think we passed the hotel manager, probably heading home. A lot of employees live on the island, don't they?"

Mr. Browning concurred, "Yes, I think some of the staff went by. We were taking our time on the beach, enjoying walking in the surf."

"It's so nice to just relax," Mrs. Browning tipped up her glass to get the last drop. "Oh, Harry, do you remember that person who nearly ran us down on the dunes?"

"Ran you down?" Mia exclaimed.

"Oh yes. You remember, Harry. We'd just left the lit part of the beach for the dunes and were slowly letting our eyes adjust to the dark so we'd see the owls. Someone ran right past us, dressed in black. They made me jump a foot," she informed Mia. "They were running on the dunes, right over the boardwalks."

"Was it that night?" Mr. Browning questioned.

"Well, I think it was. I doubt they saw us since we were standing still and it was dark except for the moonlight. They were cutting across the dunes right in front of us."

"Yes, you're right. I don't think they ever did see us."

"Can you remember what they looked like?" Mia asked eagerly.

"No, just a fast shape in black, running a foot or two away," Mrs. Browning shook her head owlishly.

"Maybe how tall they were? Were they thin or fat?"

"Well now, they couldn't have run that fast if they were fat, could they, Harry?" She looked at her husband for confirmation.

He added, thinking hard, "I'd say around my height, give or take. Not very short, not too tall. Moving, it's hard to tell."

He continued thoughtfully, "That was the night of the murder, wasn't it? I guess we'd better call the police in the morning, honey." He nodded at Mia and stood up, deftly steadying his wife. "I'm much obliged for you pointing that out, Mrs. Spinel. I hope you have a good night." They slowly made their way back to the hotel.

Mia sat for a few minutes, looking out at the dark dunes. It wouldn't be easy to bypass hotel security cameras, but she thought if you planned out your route carefully, you could walk across the dunes, overtake Trey on the beach, and be back to the hotel without a single camera seeing you.

Hannah's cottage would be even easier. Just keep to the unlit paths, and you wouldn't be seen.

But the murderer didn't plan for the Brownings, out at night, in the dark.

10

Murder is Dangerous

Mia dressed for battle the next morning in her pink sneakers and a brilliant green embroidered blouse. She carefully brushed her hair, making sure every wave was neatly in place. Two small pink spinel earrings and bright pink lipstick completed her wardrobe. She was ready for what the day would bring.

She spent a few minutes going over paperwork, then went to breakfast.

The first person she saw at the main hotel was Captain Daniels, sitting in the lounge, watching the guests like a hawk. He spied his intended prey. "May I join you for breakfast, Ms. Mia?"

"Of course," Mia warmly agreed. "There's a small, private room off the Hammock Dining Room, if that would suit you?"

"Sounds perfect."

Dorrie took their orders and returned quickly with their meals, smoked salmon and toast with a large coffee for Captain Daniels and a plain omelette for Mia, perfectly made. She sipped her coffee with pleasure. "What can I do for you, Danny?"

He smiled at her, eyes twinkling. "It hasn't exactly escaped my notice you're managing to, um, socially interact with all my main suspects in these terrible murders."

"It is my hotel," she pointed out.

"They are my murders," he rejoined.

"So why don't we pool resources?" Mia asked adroitly.

"I want to thank you for sending the Brownings to me. I can't believe those dimwits didn't think to tell me they'd seen several people wandering around the night of the murder. All they were interested in was a great horned owl pair they had spotted."

"The idea of the pair of them running around in the dark looking for owl nests," Mia rolled her eyes. "I hope they don't break an ankle and sue the hotel."

"So Hannah was definitely on the dunes that night." Danny made a note. "That confirms the theory she was blackmailing the murderer."

"And there was someone else running around on the dunes as well. Did they have a better description this morning?"

"Unfortunately, their description didn't get us much farther. All they knew was someone dark ran past them in the dark. A medium size shadow, nothing more." He shook his head. "The only new information we really have is they have to be healthy enough to run—which almost anyone could be if they had a good enough reason. They can't be very short, tall or fat."

"It cuts out Harold Stone as a suspect for the runner, at least. He's so out of shape enough running would give him a heart attack. And he's fat enough to notice, even in the dark."

"Possibly. Or possibly the night runner has nothing at all to do with the murders. Lots of people exercise at night."

"Not running in the dark on the dunes, they don't. Can you imagine how quickly you'd turn an ankle?" Mia said definitively.

"However, I certainly want to keep Harold Stone in the picture as a possible murderer," she continued. "Let me tell you why Trey must have been blackmailing him."

When she finished, Danny told her, "I'd better have another talk with Mr. Stone." He looked at his notes, "He was definitely outside the night of Trey Sulley's murder. The odd thing is, I don't have his key card opening his door either night or any cameras or people seeing him the night of Hannah Winley's murder."

"You don't have to go through the lobby to get outside," Mia pointed out. "If you used the side stairs, you could avoid the lobby altogether."

"Yes, it would be easy to exit the hotel, but how could you get back into the building without using your key card?" He tapped his pen on the table. "I'll need to think on that."

"During the day, the main building doors are open in good weather, like we've had lately. They are within sight of the concierge and other employees. As long as they knew a person belonged, the hospitality team might not even remember them entering. Also, people do tend to hold open doors for each other, not thinking about key cards." Mia sighed, "I wish they wouldn't do it, but we keep close track of who comes on and off the island so it doesn't matter as much here."

"That's during the day, not at midnight," he tapped his pen again. "Could he have propped open the door?"

"No, the security system would definitely notice an outside door left open." Mia thought a minute, "It wouldn't notice a room door open. You could prevent the latch from closing with a piece of tape. It would look closed but you could re-enter your room with no record of when you left or returned, since the card was never used either way."

"The key card is the only thing the system tracks?"

"Yes," Mia gave him a little smile. "It wouldn't be the first time people have done that to sneak around in a hotel. We really prefer not to know, as long as our guests are safe. Guest privacy is paramount."

"Very true," he said with a slight smile.

"So he could have reentered his room at any point in the night. There's no record of him leaving and none of returning. There's only the inescapable fact he was on the beach that night, apparently wandering around with a bottle."

"He was definitely on the beach at the time of the murder."

"He could have stayed out all night and returned with the beachgoers in the morning," Mia suggested. "As long as he stayed away from cameras and the part of the beach Trey's body was found, no one would notice an early morning beachgoer. He could have repeated the process the night of Hannah's death."

"He would have been filmed on the terrace or entering a side door, though." He tapped his pen, "I'll get Sergeant Waters to review the footage from that night, looking for Harold Stone or one of the other suspects, entering the building but not leaving it that morning."

"It would work for everyone staying in the main building, not the cottages," Mia pointed out.

"Works for me. That's where most of my suspects are right now." He sighed heavily, "The only one in the cottages was Hannah Winley, and she's dead, poor soul."

"Another suspect is Sissy Collinsworth," Mia told him with authority.

"She was on the beach that night. She also had hotel business dealing with Mr. Sulley. Any other reason?"

"I've pulled together figures from two of her previous charity events. She held one at the Spinel Boston and one at the St. Johns in San Francisco."

"Isn't that where Trey Sulley worked last?" Danny asked with interest.

"It is indeed," Mia told him. "And according to the manager, Trey Sulley frequently met with her to organize the event."

"Is that so?" He scribbled a note. "Interesting."

"And the numbers posted on the Green Environmental Charity's web site do not agree with the hotel records of the event expenses."

"Really?" He glanced up sharply. She had definitely caught his interest.

"I can give you the Spinel Hotel information, of course, but I think you should call the St. Johns and request the other information directly from them. The manager let me see it in strict privacy. He's one of my old employees," she twinkled at him.

"Of course he is," he snorted a laugh. "Doesn't matter. Warrants are easier to get in a murder case, especially when we know what to look for." He looked at her, "So I get she's cheating the charity? Or the charity patrons? But how?"

"She's claiming the costs of holding the event are much higher than the hotel actually charges. For instance, our standard charity discount is not deducted from the costs posted." She made a revolted face. "No wonder she was nagging me for a bigger percentage off. To steal from an environmental charity. Just despicable."

She continued, "Everything seems above board on the charity's website. They clearly have no idea Sissy has given them false receipts so they're posting it online, trying to be transparent about how much money the event brings in. Only someone who worked for the hotel and had access to the original receipts could compare the two amounts and realize just how different they are."

"Just how much are we talking about?"

"Well, Sissy is their chief fundraiser, so I imagine this is not the only scam she's pulling. However, it seems to be about a thirty percent markup on the costs, which fits with not allowing for the charity deduction or any other cost saving measures we and hotels like the St. Johns try to help charity events along with." Mia smiled, "We have to turn a profit, but we can also use the tax deduction so it works out. So she'd profit at least one hundred thousand per large event. Sissy also stays at a very nice hotel for a week or two for free, paid for by the charity."

He whistled. "One hundred thousand dollars? With a free vacation? And that's only one event a year, huh? Not a bad haul." He wrote in his notebook. "I'll interview Ms. Collinsworth first, then call her boss."

Mia nodded, "Since he's posting the information, I doubt he's in on the scam."

"Not likely," he agreed. "Trey worked with her directly at two hotels. All he would have to do is look at their website."

"It sounds like she's an experience to work with, to put it mildly, so he would have remembered at least some of the numbers. It would be easy enough to get the rest. I don't know if he asked for the Boston Spinel's information, but it would be a fairly standard practice at Spinel when working with the same charity. Having access to previous event files can save a lot of time."

"And that is a motive and means for murder." He closed his notebook with a crisp slap. "Thanks, Mia."

"You're very welcome," she smiled at him. "I have a great interest in cleaning up this mess."

"I know," he hesitated.

"Sullivan would know where Ms. Collinsworth is," she gently hinted.

"Thanks," he said, already striding out of the room.

She finished her breakfast and planned the rest of her day. She had things to do.

Mia knocked on Sam and Rebecca's door a few minutes later. They already had a visitor, Sylvie, sitting at the round table with Sam with a laptop between them.

"Hi," he waved. "I saw Sylvie on my run this morning and dragged her here. We're having a war room meeting."

"He says he can get me out of my contract," Sylvie said gratefully, her eyes brimming with hopeful tears.

"I said I think I can get you out of it," Sam corrected. "Let's not get too caught up yet. One step at a time." He paged down the document deliberately, making notes on a legal pad.

Sylvie smiled at Mia, "I feel like life is full of so many possibilities right now." She gently swung her new hair from side to side, enjoying the feel of it brushing her cheeks. "I just know it's all going to work out." She looked at her watch, "However, I do need to work with Harold in about fifteen minutes. It's still my job."

Sam nodded, "If you could send me a copy of this," he paged through, "and this, I'll get started."

"Now Sam," Rebecca said, clearly torn.

"I'll work for about an hour and have a more accurate answer for you," he said, looking at Rebecca. "Then my lovely wife and I are going sailing."

"Thanks," Sylvie said. "I know it's awful to ask you to work on your vacation."

"This vacation has not been exactly what we expected," Sam said dryly. "Helping a great writer write the books she'd like to is a treat for me."

"I agree," Rebecca said warmly.

Mia rose to go as Sylvie headed out the door.

"Mia, that was a wonderful boat ride last night. Billy and his grandson were so much fun. We even caught a few fish." Rebecca said in her warm honey voice, "Thank you so much for setting that up for us."

"Any time," Mia told her.

Sam asked, "Do you know any more about the case?"

"A bit," Mia reassured. "Since Harold Stone was on the beach that night, it's possible he killed Trey."

"Blackmailed about our friendly ghostwriter?" Rebecca asked.

Mia held her hands out indecisively, "Possibly."

"His not actually writing his most popular books would be a very good motive. I would think sales would plummet."

"Yes," Mia agreed. "I also think Sissy Collinsworth, with the Green Environmental Charity, would be another possibility. She's been skimming money from the events."

"Really?" Sam asked in disgust. "So it's down to us three suspects?"

"Sam, I can't seriously consider you a suspect," Mia said. "The Brownings and Francisco were also on the beach that night."

"You can't seriously suspect that nice birdwatching couple?" Rebecca asked.

"No, but Danny is checking into their background information, bank accounts and such. Sweet old couples can also be murderers if there's a motive. And they seem to like wandering around at night."

"Owling, they told me," Rebecca said. "They were very excited about the birds here." She giggled slightly.

"They're so cute, with the big hiking boots and cameras." She looked at Sam with adoring eyes, "I hope we do stuff like that when we're old."

"I hope we get to," Sam said dispiritedly.

"And I just can't imagine Francisco killing Trey for firing him," Mia said loudly. "Changing jobs happens constantly in his industry. It might set him back for a little bit, but that's it."

Sam said, "It still might be enough motive."

"It might be, but I don't believe it is," Mia told him. "He seems very dedicated, but his goal is not to work his way up Michelin stars but to eventually create his own restaurant. He's an incredibly talented young chef who would be an asset to any restaurant. I just don't think a small setback like being fired from one restaurant would hurt him." She sighed, "but it might make a very young man mad enough to kill."

"People aren't always logical," Sam said pedantically. "I've been thinking about the night Mrs. Winley was killed. I can't get past the shape being just a shadow, but it was moving very fast. It still could have been a deer. I don't see how it could possibly have been slow moving Harold Stone." He paused a moment, then continued. "You know, I was pretty upset that night, but when I went over things, I think there was something in the bushes near Mrs. Winley's cottage." He closed his eyes, putting himself back to that night. "I walked around the hotel straight to the beach from the parking lot. It was very dark on the side of the building, and the sounds of the palmettos scratching gave me the heebie-jeebies," he shivered. "So I walked to the lit area pretty fast and down by the side path to the beach. I passed right by Mrs. Winley's cottage. I felt like there were eyes watching me the whole time until I got to the beach. I walked down the beach until I saw that Collinsworth woman, then about faced and went the other way."

"That's very unlike you," Rebecca said, surprised. "I'm usually the one seeing things in shadows." She turned to Mia, "I always make him walk our dog last thing at night. I get to thinking something is out there, waiting to get me." She softly laughed at herself.

"That's interesting," Mia said. "I expect you heard the murderer."

Sam shuddered involuntarily. "I expect I did. Odd, how we react to things."

"Our ancient brains are sometimes wiser than our modern ones." Mia opened the door, "I'll leave you to it."

When Mia left, Rebecca looked at Sam. He avoided her eyes, frowning down at his notes. "Hi, honey," she said loudly.

He looked at her, then muttered, "I've gotten us in a mess."

"You certainly have," Rebecca agreed. She came over to him, moving his papers out of the way. Wrapping her arms around his neck, she sat in his lap.

"I don't even know why Captain Daniels hasn't arrested me," he looked into her brown eyes mournfully.

"I do," Rebecca told him. "You're not guilty." She looked at him with complete confidence.

"How does he know that?"

"It's pretty obvious you're not a killer. And Mia thinks you're innocent."

"So?"

"Captain Daniels isn't stupid. He worked here when Mia was manager, you know. No one who worked under Mia would think her judgment was that wrong."

"You think?" Sam was clearly trying to believe her, but couldn't.

"Trust me on this one." Rebecca slid her long tanned leg along his. "She'll find out. She's like a terrier—there's no way someone gets away with murder at her hotel." She tapped his notebook, "You take care of the project she gave you—she'll take care of the murderer. Trust me."

"I have something else I'd like to take care of first," Sam caught up her hair in his hands and kissed her.

Mia went to the spa in the late afternoon, setting up a hair appointment after her massage. Jasmine massaged her neck and shoulders. "A lot of stress, Ms. Mia."

Mia agreed, enjoying the soothing strokes of the hot stones taking away all the little aches of the day. "That feels wonderful, Jasmine."

"You'll feel better after this, that's for sure."

Mia lay there in bliss, letting Jasmine's soothing touch and relaxed Southern drawl tell her about the spa that day.

When the massage was over, she just lay there for a few minutes, relaxing and thinking. The calm sound of the waterfall surrounded the room. Voices were muffled; nothing from the outside world intruded. She felt that she was in a warm safe cocoon. It was almost time for her to emerge, armed with the truth.

When she finally arrived at the salon, she was the only guest. Mr. Henry bustled around her, clever fingers closely examining every strand of her hair, frowning energetically.

She burst out laughing. "Henry, I get my hair done at every one of our hotels to check them out. I know you're better at it."

"Humph," he grunted.

"Why do you think I come here at least once a year?" Mia teased him, "To see you, of course." And the Spinel Grand Island always felt like coming home.

Henry still frowned, but she could see the grin underneath. "A little color, perhaps?"

"Just bit of a touch up. We can't have people thinking I'm not a natural blonde, can we?"

"Well, of course not. I'd never dream of such a thing."

"You'll be here another week, won't you? I'd prefer to do color today and wait one more week for shaping." Henry was all business now.

"Yes, I think I might be here a little longer than planned." Mia had had a long talk this afternoon with her children all telling her to come home right now and stay there and fix things, all at the same time. It had been a very long talk and she'd deliberately muted her phone afterwards.

"I'd think so, with that horrible murder," Henry shuddered dramatically. "And on our beach."

He started working on her hair, efficiently dying the roots while gossiping in his soft Southern accent. "Now, I had no trouble at all believing someone would kill Trey one day. I just wish it hadn't happened here." Grimacing a little, he changed the subject, "Did Sylvie enjoy her new look?"

"I saw her this morning, and she looked beautiful. I think she's going to be so much happier from now on." She would be if Mia had anything to do with it.

"It's funny how a hairstyle can make all the difference to a woman. Men, they don't care so much. They like looking good, but if they know who they are, they don't like change. With women now, the right hairstyle completely changes their outlook on life."

"It does, doesn't it?" Mia had known who she was and the hairstyle that matched her personality for decades.

"Take that woman you came to the spa with the other day, Allison Jayton. I fixed her hair where it covers that ugly scarring all over her right cheek." He smiled in pride, "Changing the part and a few layers and she is a stunner."

"She is beautiful, isn't she?" Mia said thoughtfully. "I didn't realize you were responsible for the hairstyle."

"Oh, she'd read about me in some magazine," Henry coughed discretely. "So she came the first day she was here."

"That's nice," Mia agreed. "She said she was doing things she'd only read about."

"Good to have some fun," Henry said with enthusiasm. "Now that Sissy Collinsworth, I wouldn't touch her hair with a ten foot pole. No respect for style or herself."

"Did she come in?" Mia asked, interested.

"Yes, but I took one look at her and turned her over to my assistant, Maggie." Henry smiled, "There are some things an artist just can't do. She complained every step of the cut. Told Maggie she was doing everything wrong. Like Maggie would! Even with all that, Maggie made her look fabulous." He puffed out his chest, "And, my dear, do you know what she did as she left?"

"No, what?" Mia tried hard not to laugh.

"She pulled her fingers through her hair, totally changing the part and moving everything," Henry said in shock. "It looked like she'd just stepped off a boat in a storm. Maggie nearly cried."

"Oh dear," Mia tried to inject the proper note of horrified shock. "Some people."

"Indeed," Henry said majestically. He finished up a last few touches. "Off you go, my dear. And I'll see you next week for shaping."

Mia looked at herself in the mirror with pleasure. "I love the little touches of caramel you've done."

"Even with ash blondes, you want a bit of color and depth," Henry told her.

"Thank you," Mia slid off the chair, smiling. She tried very hard not to touch her gorgeous new hair as she left the room.

The air outside was a physical shock, dense and muggy, enveloping her completely. She wandered into the lobby, sitting in the corner wing chair and taking in the room. It was the same room. Nothing had changed but the people. Hardly anyone sat in the lobby now and the few who did, looked at each other warily.

She noticed Billy over in the corner, keeping an unobtrusive eye on the entire room from behind a book. She nodded briefly to him and he responded with a quick wink, going back to surveying the room. Maria must have him on duty. Billy always turned up where he was most useful.

Dorrie came up to her, "Hi, Ms. Mia. May I bring you something?" Her brittle smile was professional, not openly cheerful as usual.

"Thanks, Dorrie. I'd love a sweet tea."

"And a biscuit?" Dorrie asked, with a tiny trace of a real smile.

"Absolutely," Mia agreed heartily, more to acknowledge Dorrie's thoughtfulness than for the biscuit.

Sissy Collinsworth came into the lobby and spotted her immediately, making a beeline for her chair. "How dare you tell the police I was stealing from the Green Environmental Charity? I'll sue you for this," she accused loudly enough for the entire room to hear.

Well, Mia could hide or give the lobby something else to talk about besides the murders. With an inward smile, she decided to give the room a show.

Her voice clearly penetrated the entire room, cutting through all background noise, reaching into the bar. "My dear, I just pointed out the financial information published on," she raised her voice more, "the Green

218

Environmental Charity's website about the events you set up and the actual financial information with my hotel did not agree. The charity reported your event expenses as at least thirty percent higher than they actually were."

The room became enthralled by the theater. The room was hushed, listening avidly for Sissy's reply. People paused, no longer in a hurry to move through the lobby to their rooms.

Sissy blustered, "I could sue!"

Mia ignored the empty threat. "I believe that ends up being at least a hundred thousand dollar discrepancy for the Green Environmental Charity, on that event alone. I believe you are their chief fundraiser with several events per year?"

Suddenly noticing the intently listening room, Sissy said nothing. Mia saw Sullivan purposefully moving closer. Billy had put his book down.

Mr. Browning came up, mint julep in hand. "Is that right?"

Sissy bluffed, "Absolutely not."

He said meaningfully, "I'm one of the Green Environmental Charity's trustees, you know."

Mia broke in, "I'd be glad to give you any information the Spinel Hotels have. All I know is there is a discrepancy between published information and my hotel's records. Your accounting should be able to handle the rest."

Sissy yapped shrilly, "You can't do that!"

Mr. Browning said, ignoring Sissy, "I'd like to see that."

"I'd be happy to get you a copy tomorrow morning," Mia said.

"You can't do that," Sissy whispered.

"If it's no trouble, I'd like to see it tonight." He smiled, "I don't like the thought of sleeping on a hundred thousand dollar discrepancy for a charity I'm a trustee for."

"Of course. It's no trouble at all."

Sullivan respectfully but firmly took hold of Sissy's arm. "I'll escort you to your room."

"You can't do that," she lashed out at him with her other hand and he caught it in a surprisingly strong grip.

"Ma'am, I'm choosing to believe that was an accident after a bit too much to drink." He wheeled her toward the elevator. Sissy had no choice but to follow.

Mr. Browning went back to his wife, frowning. Sullivan returned to his desk, looking at the guests in the lobby glumly. He was clearly uncertain how to improve the mood.

Mia quickly texted the information request to Maria, then sat frowning. She heard guests start to talk warily, wondering if Sissy Collinsworth was a murderer. Good, it would make them feel safer, she thought.

With a flourish, Dorrie placed the shining silver tray beside her, wafting the buttery biscuit smell toward her. Mia quietly asked, "How are things?"

Dorrie leaned in to whisper, "The guests aren't enjoying themselves, like usual. I think because Mrs. Winley was a guest, they're worried."

Mia nodded thoughtfully. "I'll think of something."

She motioned to Sullivan and he quickly left his desk. "What's going on?"

"A lot of requests for day trips away from the hotel," he said significantly. "There's a big storm coming through tonight so I've had to put a halt to the boat outings. Golf was pretty popular today, but people will be coming in from the course for dinner soon."

Mia pondered a minute, then said quietly, "We need a party in here. A sense of festivity. The carefree vacation these people want." She motioned Dorrie over and whispered. "It might not hurt if you gossiped a little that Mrs. Winley was on the beach the night of the first murder and probably witnessed it, which led to her death. No sense in other guests worrying about them being next."

Dorrie nodded understanding, "Rumor mill starts working now," she whispered back with a small smile.

Mia continued in her normal voice, "A storm coming? So let's do some drinks and nibbles here. Maybe some ginger juleps, mint juleps, and of course, champagne. Then, classic nibbles. Cheese straws, biscuits with butter and honey, some pastries. Francisco will be in his element here, just ask him. We need to enjoy this night. Get the pianist in here," she nodded at the grand piano in the corner, "Let's play some music that makes your toes tap."

Sullivan and Dorrie went off. Dorrie returned in a minute with several other waiters in tow, bearing the start of the party supplies. Mia smiled as she saw Dorrie and the other waiters bending confidentially to proffer gossip and free drinks, leaving a wave of cheerful relief and hushed conversations in their wake. The pianist started playing old jazz and new dance music, alternating to create a party atmosphere. As the drinks flowed and people nibbled, moods improved. More people wandered into the lobby to get a snack or glass of champagne, then stayed to enjoy the happy mood.

Mia smiled. This was the fun part of running a hotel. Her feet tapped to the music and she sipped her iced tea in pleasure. She loved impromptu parties. They were always the best kind.

Two young couples laughed and danced in the center of the room. They clearly didn't know whether to do modern dance moves or the Charleston to the fast jazz, but they were having fun in the process.

The elderly man resting in the corner chair perked up at the music. He hoisted himself to his feet and held out his hand to his youngest granddaughter, "May I have this dance, young lady?"

The little girl laughed and reached up high to hold his hands and dance. The smiles on young and old were beautiful.

She saw Maria come in, nod approvingly when she saw the room, and head to Mr. and Mrs. Browning. She spoke with them for a minute, then came over to Mia. "Nice party," she said, looking uplifted along with the room's mood. "I delivered the information you instructed to the Browning's room personally, as well as a fruit basket."

"They'll have something to feed to the birds, then," Mia smiled. "How are things?"

"Pretty good, considering," Maria told her. "Most people still here aren't leaving. I've had a few more cancellations, but no one is going to change a June wedding in the South now. There are more calls asking if the," she coughed, "problems continue, could they get an extension on the full refund period." She looked at Mia, "I've assured them they can."

"Good." Mia gestured at the room. "Now relax a minute and enjoy the party."

Maria shook her head, "Things to do right now. A personal touch makes all the difference. You've done my work for me here," her smile encompassed the cheerful room.

"Little things make all the difference," Mia agreed. "I'll see you later, then."

Billy came over to her chair, book in hand, as Maria hastened away. "Like some company?"

"I would indeed," Mia twinkled at him. "Take a seat. What are you up to tonight? And where's your lovely Jolie?"

"She's home safe. Maria asked me to stay tonight with the storm coming and the troubles. Might be useful. No matter to me," he shrugged noncommittally.

"I'm glad," Mia told him. "I have a few things I'd like to discuss with you."

They talked for a few minutes about a few more ideas she'd had.

"This party certainly cheered things up, Ms. Mia," he encouraged, standing up. "If we do a little more of the same sort of thing, we'll be back to normal in no time."

"I agree, Billy." Mia looked around at the lively room. She saw couples toasting each other with champagne. Over in the corner, that nice old man was now holding court with a silver cupped mint julep happily in hand, grandchildren with fizzy fruit punches and cookies encircling him. A newly arrived wedding party greeted each other, long parted friends catching up.

Allison sat down next to her, clearly enjoying the merriment. "What a celebration! This is fun, Mia. Did you set it up?"

"I may have had a hand in it," Mia gave her a sly wink.

"Grand Island seems like such a nice, old fashioned hotel." She gestured at the tiered silver trays of tiny pastries and the grand piano. "It reminds me of," she broke off, then continued with her voice a little harsh, "better times."

"Like at the St. Johns?" Mia asked kindly.

"Yes, we used to go every week," she broke off again. "How did you know?"

"The manager there, John Blount, is an old friend of mine. I was asking him about Sissy Collinsworth..." she trailed off.

"I was there for that," Allison gave a brief smile.

"And he said how lovely you and your partner were and how much he missed you both at afternoon tea."

"He said that?" Allison asked in surprise. "I wouldn't have thought he'd remember us." She smiled wanly. "We had so much fun there."

"He remembered you both very well." Mia smiled compassionately at her. "We've all lost someone and

224

blamed ourselves when it wasn't really our fault, my dear. You have to move on and accept what happened."

"Yes, well," Allison choked. She admitted in a harsh voice. "I was driving that night. It was my fault."

"Oh, my dear, you know it was just a terrible accident." Mia looked at her sympathetically. "You know it wasn't your fault."

Allison stumbled to her feet, trying not to cry in public. "I have to go."

Mia watched her stumble to the elevator, concerned, but not wanting to intrude. The party which had been so much fun a moment ago sounded discordant and off. She sighed. She'd done what she could.

Her view was suddenly blocked by Harold Stone, his fat paunch at eye level. "Where's Sylvie?"

"Excuse me?" Mia disliked craning her neck up, especially to such an unprepossessing view.

His face was red and bloated, spittle at the corners of his mouth. "I know you have my assistant. How am I supposed to get a book written without her?"

"I have no idea," Mia replied coldly. "I would assume you can write it."

"Of course I damn well can," Harold yelled drunkenly. "I just need my assistant."

"I don't know where Sylvie is," she told him. "Why don't you go to your room and I'll send her to you as soon as I find her?"

"You'll find her?" he asked Mia. He looked more upset than drunk now.

"I'll send her to your room, Mr. Stone, as soon as I find her."

"I don't know if she'll come. I don't remember," he rambled. "She may not come," he finished, sadly. "And my books. My beautiful books."

"I'll make sure she gets your message, Mr. Stone."

The cheerful crowd made a channel for him to pass, then closed behind him, hardly noticing the famous writer had passed through the room. The piano music continued its happy party music.

Mia felt tired and alone at the party. It was time for her to go. She made her way over to Sullivan. "At seven o'clock, slowly start winding up the party so people will shift to dinner."

He nodded, looking at his watch. "No problem."

"Then tell the pianists to keep up party music in the dining rooms, keep things lively through dinner. They'll know what to do."

"You're not staying?"

"No, I think I'll have dinner at my cottage, have an early night." She smiled brightly, patting her hair, "I don't want to mess up Mr. Henry's work with the storm."

"It does look gorgeous," Sullivan complemented her. "Off you go before the rain, then. Would you like to order dinner first?"

"Just soup and a salad," Mia requested. "Thanks."

"No problem." The concierge looked over her shoulder as a guest approached. Mia quietly left the party, pleased with the gaiety she'd created tonight.

11

A Dark and Stormy Night

The storm was building outside, the air felt heavy and almost suffocating. Under the rapidly darkening sky, guests hurried to the hotel for dinner before the rain started. As distant thunder rumbled, Mia was glad she'd decided to have dinner at her cottage.

She changed her strappy sandals for cosy slippers, made some evening preparations and looked out at the dark sky. The storm was coming on quickly. She saw Dorrie running with the room service cart and opened the door wide. The rain was just starting in great fat drops, heralding the storm's arrival.

Dorrie bent to get the tablecloth to cover the table, but Mia stopped her, "Honey, leave the cart and get it in the morning. You need to run for it right now."

Dorrie flashed her a quick smile and ran, disappearing quickly into the dark.

Mia closed the door on the rain. She gave the tablecloth a crisp snap and spread it on the table, set the table, then placed the covered dishes on it. Dimming the lights, she pulled two heavy silver candlesticks out of the cart and lit them, then poured herself a glass of bubbly. The many dishes Francisco sent smelled appetizing. She wondered what treats he'd made for her to try tonight.

Sitting down, she left the curtains open on her little courtyard to watch the storm.

The courtyard was an island of relative calm among whipping palm trees, protected by the high privacy walls. Leaves blew past the French doors, swirling next to the walls. Rain splattered the terrace and a chair moved in the wind. Even through the rising storm, she could hear the bricks scraping under the chair legs. She shivered and said to herself, "I do not want to go out there tonight."

"You're not going to," a voice said behind her.

She looked up and met Allison Jayton's eyes in the reflection. "Hello, Cindy."

"You don't seem surprised," Allison said in confusion. "Why aren't you surprised?" She abruptly realized what Mia had said. "Why are you calling me Cindy?"

"You weren't the one driving, Cindy. Allison was." Mia said sadly. "It wasn't your fault."

"It was!" Cindy Silvers said in despair. "We were arguing and she took her eyes off the road to look at me.

It was raining so hard. Just like tonight." Her eyes went to the rain outside, then back to Mia.

"It still wasn't your fault, my dear."

"The car hit a puddle and skidded. The car hit everything, spinning around and around. Everything crashed into us." She sobbed, "I don't remember anything else until I woke up in the hospital."

"And they called you Allison," Mia stated.

"And they called me Allison," Cindy repeated, collapsing onto the chair opposite Mia.

"It wasn't your fault," Mia repeated.

"My face was all," she shuddered. "They thought I was Allison. They'd started the surgeries." She stroked her face, remembering. "So many surgeries. I wasn't Cindy anymore. I couldn't see Cindy in the mirror anymore. So I became Allison."

"And Allison wasn't dead, that way."

"No, I could look in the mirror and see her still." Cindy looked at her reflection in the glass for reassurance. "Cindy's dead, not Allison." She swung her long black hair, letting it fall on her shoulders where she could see it clearly. "I'm Allison."

"Oh, my dear," Mia said, heartbroken for her.

"I am not your dear," Cindy screamed, her voice harsh with tears. "I am Allison Jayton, a wealthy, independent woman. I don't need anyone." She said firmly, "A survivor."

"You are a survivor, Cindy," Mia's voice was gentle.

"Don't call me that!" she lashed out. "I'm Allison."

Mia's voice was calm, "Of course, Allison." She went on in a butterfly soft voice, "Did Trey recognize you? Blackmail you?"

"He did," she said angrily. "He said he recognized my laugh. How could he?"

Mia remembered Allison's high distinctive laugh. "You have a beautiful laugh, my dear."

"He was an idiot. He'd made a pass at me at the St. Johns. I got him fired for it, nasty creep. Why would you hire a manager like that?" Cindy asked furiously.

"I didn't hire him," Mia said, with distinct agreement. "I'm very sorry, so very sorry he blackmailed you."

"Yes, well, he was sorry too, but it didn't make any difference," Cindy's bark of laughter was very different from her happy laugh.

"You stole a rope from the boat shop, didn't you?" Mia told her. "And climbed down from your balcony."

Cindy stared at her in shock, "How did you know that?"

"Oh, honey," Mia said in despair. "Of course I know. He'd threatened you, didn't he? And you were already hurting so badly."

Cindy scoffed, "Me hurting? He was the one hurting. He thought since he'd recognized me I'd have to sleep with him and pay him money." She shuddered at the thought, then her voice went softly terrible, "He thought I'd killed Allison." She repeated, still shocked at the thought, "Killed Allison?" She continued ferociously, banging her fist on the table and making the candles flicker wildly. "He was scum, lower than scum, and I stabbed him dead."

"Where did you get the knife?"

Cindy bragged, "I grabbed it from that drunk Harold's table the night before. He always has steak. The next night, I put it back next to his steak plate, shiny clean. The waiter just thought they'd laid an extra knife."

Mia said with arrogant certainty, "My waiters never lay extra knives."

"Whatever," Cindy told her. "No one noticed," she said smugly.

"True." Mia thought a second. "But I know Sergeant Waters wouldn't have missed it in her search."

"Yeah, she didn't much like me, did she?" Cindy smiled proudly, "I left it in my tennis bag, in the gym lockers."

"Clever." Mia continued, "And you killed Hannah because she'd known you growing up."

"Yeah, we were on the cheerleading team together in high school. She was pretty and greedy even then." Cindy smirked. "Always after the richest boys she could find."

"Did she see you the night of Trey's murder? I know she was on the dunes."

"Absolutely everyone was on the dunes that night. The night I pick to get rid of Trey and everyone's wandering around in the dark." Cindy said indignantly.

"I nearly ran into that old couple, then on the way back I did run into Hannah. I knocked her flat." Cindy shook her head, "I knew Hannah wouldn't tell on me—Trey was blackmailing her too, so his death stopped his blackmail. But after she realized she'd be out of money when her husband kicked her ass out for sleeping around, she came to me for money." Cindy's face was disgusted. "She never cared about anything but money and men, even in high school."

"Even with your newfound wealth you couldn't have kept her level of spending up for long." Mia shifted slightly in her seat, glancing out at the storm. It was at full strength now, wind howling. The lights flickered, but stayed on.

"I worked hard for my money. She married for it," Cindy said indignantly. "I bet you still don't know how I killed Hannah," Cindy bragged.

Mia smiled grimly, "You killed her with her own sleeping pills. You broke into her house through the back window when she was gone during the day and grabbed enough pills to do the trick. Very clever again. I'm surprised they didn't think it was suicide after the scene she made at dinner." She asked curiously, "But how did you get the Scotch? Did you steal it from the bar?"

"No, I didn't steal it," Cindy said, clearly upset by the accusation. She boasted, "Getting the Scotch was tricky, I didn't have a car and I didn't want to draw attention to myself by leaving. And I couldn't buy it from the hotel." She repeated, "I didn't steal it."

Mia could guess, but she'd prefer Cindy to keep talking. She was sure she knew what Cindy planned for Mia when she stopped talking. "So how did you get it?"

"I got it from Trey's house!" Cindy laughed, braying her high piercing laugh. "They'd already searched it and I remembered he had some awfully nice bottles in his liquor cabinet." She shook her head at Mia, "You really need to keep a tighter eye on your staff. I'm sure he took most of them from the hotel."

"I'm sure you're right."

"It was a very nice bottle of Scotch. I simply mixed in the pills and left it for dear Hannah's nightcap." Her hands clenched and unclenched spasmodically on the table, wrinkling the crisp white cloth. "Easy as pie."

"Very simple."

Cindy reached for the silver candlestick, turning it in her hand. She gently blew out the flame. "You know I have to kill you now."

"I know you're going to try," Mia said calmly. She met Cindy's eyes with no fear. "My dear, it has to stop somewhere, you know."

"Why would it?" Cindy asked in Allison's voice.

"You can't go on killing everyone who knows you're Cindy."

"I am Allison!" her voice rang the room and she swept the candlestick toward Mia's head in a death blow.

Mia ducked to the floor and rolled away, getting back to her feet as quickly as her yoga practice had prepared her for.

At the same time, the curtain billowed and Billy leaped out, tackling Cindy. Cindy struggled, but didn't have a chance against the wiry strength of the small man. He held her face down with one hand and pulled up her arm in a painful hold. She wailed, high and piteous.

Danny jerked the closet door open, a few seconds too late to help Billy with the takedown. Billy relinquished his hold on Cindy only when Danny's cuffs went on.

She still wailed, rocking and keening a high undulating cry, in deep grief. Mia shuddered, leaning against the wall for strength to remain standing. She asked, "Did you get that?"

"We got everything on both cameras," Danny told her in grim satisfaction, not letting the broken woman out of his grip. He said formally, "Cindy Silvers, I'm arresting you for..."

"I'm not Cindy! I'm Allison!" She screamed at him. Billy balanced on the balls of his feet, ready to take her down again.

Danny looked at Mia for help. She shrugged. Then he quickly read Cindy her rights, adding Allison's name to the mix. He read them one more time, her screaming, with just her name. "One of those should do it," he said with finality. He called for Sergeant Waters to bring the car around from where she waited, just off the island.

When the sergeant got there, they marched Cindy Silvers to the police car and drove off, sirens blaring into the calm after the storm.

Billy and Mia were left standing in the room, staring at each other.

Billy's voice shook ever so slightly, "Reminds me of a psycho guy I arrested in the Marines once. Went nuts."

"She did, didn't she? Poor girl."

"Poor girl? Nuts," Billy said firmly. "She killed two people."

Carefully, Mia moved away from the wall that had been the only thing keeping her upright. "Not very nice people though. They were blackmailers."

"She tried to kill you, Mia," Billy said in disbelief. "You trapped her, got her to confess to the murders on video."

"I know I did," Mia sighed heavily. "She had to be stopped. I still feel so sorry for her."

She noticed the covered dishes still waiting on the table. Straightening her shoulders, she deliberately set out another place. "Let's eat."

12

And Now We Feast

A few nights later, they celebrated. A private dining room was reserved and Mia happily spent an hour conferring with Francisco in the kitchen over what delicacies to serve. Silver gleamed in soft candlelight and multiple plates at every place hinted of the extravagances to come.

Peacock blue draperies, mirrors and ornate creamy plaster mouldings decorated the large room. Mia's dress of soft silk reflected the rooms colors beautifully. Her diamond encircled blue spinel necklace and earrings twinkled under the soft light. As her guests came in the large paneled doors, Mia greeted them warmly.

Maria and her husband arrived first, Maria fussing over the table details one last time. Javier caught up with Mia while they waited for the next guests, telling her all about Jake's heroic exploits at his last baseball game. Mia smiled and thought of her sons sliding into home plate.

Sylvie came on her own, shiny hair bouncing, freshly styled by Mr. Henry. Mia had shopped with Sylvie to find the perfect navy dress for almost any occasion. She looked like the successful author she soon would be. Sam had fired off her parting shots to Harold Stone's lawyers.

After finishing the last book she would ever ghostwrite, it was time to write her own. Mia had set her up with an agent friend of hers. Sylvie would be more concerned about which publisher to choose than if she would be published. And Sam would check any contracts before she signed them.

Danny and his wife, Erica, arrived, he, tall and handsome in his gray Sunday suit and she, cheerfully round in flowered silk. He introduced his wife to Mia with pride. "You're the reason Danny has been working around the clock," Erica told her innocently. "He did want so badly to beat you in solving the case."

Danny snorted a laugh and Mia said, "Next time, maybe."

"I hope not," Maria put in. "I never want to see a week like that here again."

Rebecca and Sam burst in the room, hurrying, adding their laughter to the room. Holding hands, they looked like the last few days had indeed been the second honeymoon they had needed.

Billy and Jolie arrived a little behind the others. "One more drop off at the airport," he told her. "A very happy couple finishing their honeymoon. I'm not sure they saw anything of the island, but they sure seemed to have had a nice honeymoon."

Rebecca blushed a little and leaned against Sam. He added, smiling at her, "Perfect place for a honeymoon."

"Absolutely," Rebecca smiled back, her heart in her eyes.

Mia had arranged for Dorrie to be their waitress tonight. She supplied them all with champagne, then waited against the wall, listening. Mia told her, "Take a glass too, Dorrie." She smiled at the girl.

They turned to their hostess. Mia said, "To happy vacations and blissful honeymoons returning to the hotel. Without you all, I might never have solved the case."

Danny muttered with good humor, "I would have." His wife tapped his arm lightly in warning. He smiled at Mia.

Mia spoke a little louder, "With your help, the murders were solved and the hotel is back to normal. To my wonderful friends, new and old, I found at the Spinel Grand Island Hotel. Let's drink to the rest of this year being the best yet!"

"I'll drink to that," Maria said with a long sip. The rest followed with happy smiles.

"Mia," Rebecca asked, "I don't understand how you knew Allison was the murderer."

"I knew she was the killer almost at once," Mia said. "It was fairly obvious Trey Sulley wasn't the type she'd be interested in, especially with such a recent loss."

"People don't always run true to type," Danny objected.

"No, and losses can make people do crazy things to run from them," Mia smiled sadly. "When she said she'd never been to the St. Johns, I thought that was odd. Anyone who would come to experience this hotel would certainly have seen the best her own city had to offer, even if she was a workaholic."

"So she was lying?" Danny questioned.

"She lied about that before the murder, so it wasn't necessarily connected with the murder." Mia took a long sip of champagne, savoring the cool bubbles and gathering her thoughts. "But it showed her distancing herself from Trey, even then. When I found out they might have known each other before, I wondered about all the plastic surgeries. The St. Johns manager said Allison was the extrovert and Cindy the quiet one. She dressed dramatically and acted that way, but she actually spent more time alone reading, running on the beach, sailing, all solo activities. She seemed nervous of making new friends. It just didn't fit until I realized that personality fit Cindy very well."

"I didn't know how to prove it until Henry told me her scarring was on the right side of her face." Mia looked at her audience for emphasis. "But if she'd been the driver, as she said, her injuries would have been on the left side of her face. The passenger of the car would have glass injuries on the right side of her face."

"It was easy to prove once we knew where to look," Danny shook his head sadly. "They'd started the surgeries before she even woke up. Allison had been to the dentist using Cindy's insurance once. She'd needed an emergency crown when they were broke and first starting the business. They'd simply continued the switch after they were successful, not bothering to change things. The dentist identified them with the records he had."

He continued, "It's a damn shame, but easy enough to understand. The purses were scrambled, and the women looked similar. About the same height, weight and both had brown hair. Allison dyed hers a dark black, but after the surgeries to keep her alive, it would have been hard to tell anything but dark brown."

Rebecca added softly, "It's not like the other woman would have been around for comparison. She was dead. Once Cindy Silvers was identified as Allison Jayton they must have just concentrated on saving her life and rebuilding her body."

Mia nodded. "I can't imagine the horror of waking up to find out your best friend is dead, and you have her face...," she shivered.

Danny told them, "She's insane, of course. Completely fell apart under questioning. She'll be locked up where she can't hurt others."

Sam added, "I know she wasn't mentally stable at the time, and so isn't responsible for her actions. However, she planned very detailed murders for an insane woman."

"The poor woman," Mia agreed sorrowfully. "But, you know, she didn't actually have to kill anyone. Trey Sulley and Hannah Winley weren't great losses to humanity, but they did have the right to live. All she had to do was say, why yes, she was Cindy Silvers. Most of her knew quite well who she was, she just refused to face it."

"True," Danny shrugged. "They were equal partners in their business with right of survivorship. All Cindy would have had to do was say the doctors made a mistake and she went a little nuts."

"I can't imagine her not being treated with great sympathy after that. And she had enough money to pay for lawyers to straighten things out." Mia shook her head. "It's terrible, but there was no reason for her to commit murder, not once, but twice. No one has the right to take another's life unless in self defense."

"Amen to that," Billy agreed. "Now we're agreed on that, let's eat!"

Mia laughed. It was time to enjoy the party.

Ms. Mia Murder Mysteries

A Gilded Age mansion on a secluded Maine island, perched on rocky cliffs overlooking the ocean, sets the scene for a classic cozy whodunit.

At the exclusive Moose Isle Inn, Ms. Mia uncovers trouble at a corporate retreat, with a bitter battle over Tisserande Linens' future. Lauren Tisserande fights to revive her Maine hometown with a new factory, but her controlling CEO husband, obsessive CFO, and suspiciously wealthy trustees conspire to stop her. Her dysfunctional sales team flatly refuses to sell the new factory's products, distracted by their own pursuits.

When murder threatens Lauren's plans, Ms. Mia unleashes her talent as an amateur sleuth, diving into the investigation with charm, wit—and a glass of champagne. No one gets away with murder at her hotels!

Check in to the adventure with Ms. Mia and Murder at Moose Isle Inn!

A stolen treasure disrupts Ms. Mia's grandest adventure yet in this delightful cozy mystery.

When an ancient flute is unearthed at The Desert Sunrise Resort, Ms. Mia seizes the chance to host a dazzling exhibit, roping in charismatic archaeologist Kyle Lee to star in a documentary. But when the flute vanishes in the middle of the night, the grand opening—and Ms. Mia's reputation—are at risk.

Armed with wit, champagne and help from her young nephew and the resort's brilliant concierge, Ms. Mia dives into a whirlwind investigation. No one gets away with murder at her hotels!

On a sun-drenched tropical paradise, Ms. Mia chases a vanishing corpse and a cunning killer in this delightful cozy murder mystery.

When a body mars the pristine beauty of the white sand beach of the Spinel Reef Resort, Ms. Mia's island getaway takes a sinister turn. When the body mysteriously disappears, she sets out to identify the murderer—and prove her sanity.

Armed with wit, charm and a splash of champagne, Ms. Mia dives into a whirlwind of tropical intrigue and hidden motives. No one gets away with murder at her resorts!

This fourth Ms. Mia Murder Mystery delivers charm, humor, and a cozy whodunit that will keep you guessing until the last wave.

Check into *Ms. Mia and Murder at the Spinel Reef Resort* for a glamorous, sun-soaked mystery, available November 1, 2025!

Ms Mia
and
Murder
on
Moose Isle

The Moose Isle Inn

Jennifer Branch

1

This Changes Everything

Lauren Tisserande Baker raised her voice over the shocked cries, "Quiet, please."

The room hushed. With one short sentence she'd changed their lives and their company completely. "Tisserande Linens is moving all production back to the United States." Every single person in the room waited anxiously to hear more.

"For a long time, I've watched our town of Megeso Point, Maine, slowly dying. I've seen the thriving town my great-grandparents and you built fade away. Buildings stand vacant, stores close. Young people leave as soon as they graduate from high school. There are no jobs to keep them here, even if they wanted to stay. I want the town I grew up—we grew up in—to be more than just an empty shell."

Lauren looked around the company cafeteria. She knew every expectant face, from summer interns to veterans of fifty years. Her hands clenched the old oak podium her grandfather had made from scrap wood, until her knuckles hurt. If she didn't make the right decisions this time, the town she loved would never recover. They trusted her. She'd never been more scared —or more determined—in her life.

Roughly clearing her throat, she dove in. "I've felt for a while the current success of Tisserande Linens, my family's company, was bought by this town's empty storefronts. I know grandparents who never see their grandchildren. Their children left here because there were no jobs. We sent those jobs offshore." Lauren choked back tears. "We sold out so we could compete in the big box stores, where price always triumphs over quality. That can't be the only way. That shouldn't be our future."

She shook her head vehemently and risked a look at the small line of management flanking her. Most of the people surrounding her frankly disapproved of her risking their well paid jobs to rehire people laid off a decade ago. They didn't understand that Lauren thought of every single person in the company, in the town, as her extended family. Most of them weren't from around here, but she'd grown up here. She'd baked cookies with their moms after school, ridden bikes on adventures, hauled lobster traps and picked apples with the people in this room. Megeso Point was her home.

Cynthia Clark, her VP of finance, tapped her pen sharply, punctuating her displeasure. Her strident voice echoed in Lauren's mind, "You'll end up ruining what's left of Tisserande. Then, no one will have a job here." Well, she was risking it all, then.

"All that is changing right now, on my watch." She spoke forcefully. "We're bringing back quality, made in the USA, made in Maine, made by us in our great town. We're rebuilding our town and our company like it should be. We're rebuilding with jobs first."

The room cheered and feet stomped wildly.

Lauren spoke over the thunderous approval. "It's not going to happen overnight, but we're doing this as fast as we can make it happen." She was gambling all Tisserande's profits, as well as most of her own capital, on the expansion. Working fast took money and lots of it.

The room stilled again. No one wanted to miss a word.

"I've devised a five year plan to bring all production back to the United States, starting with a new high end line. In two weeks, we break ground on a state of the art production facility that will provide work for an additional two hundred employees in Megeso Point by next year. That's just the start." Lauren nodded at the VP of Production, Max Davis, who gave her a quick, approving smile. "Max is already building the machines for the new line." She grinned suddenly. "That's the complicated mess in his workshop you've all been asking about. "

The room laughed a little, with relief more than mirth.

She continued, gripping the podium so hard her knuckles turned white, "The next phase will move the rest of our offshore production back home, creating more jobs for the community. With modern engineering capabilities, we can keep all of our production in-house, and improve the quality dramatically at the same time."

On her right, her husband, Paul Baker, the company president muttered sourly, "And lower the profit tremendously." He crossed his arms tightly, distancing himself from the announcement.

Ignoring him, she raised her voice. "We can make our community thrive again, and build Tisserande Linens into a better company."

"What about the old factory?" someone shouted from the back of the cafeteria.

"We have plans to refurbish it into a store," Lauren told them. "We can use it for a seconds outlet, like we used to have."

"People would drive all the way from Boston to shop," Cynthia commented grudgingly. "It brought a nice profit, from what I understand." Her pen tapping slowed slightly.

"Where's the new factory going?" a gawky kid yelled out, raising his hand, as if in school. He didn't look like he was old enough to be out of school.

"The old Malone estate, right behind the old factory. It went up for sale, zoned industrial. We're closing on it next week," Lauren said proudly. It had been the perfect location, just outside the town center. Not too far to drive during the brutal Maine winters. Not a potential eyesore in the middle of town.

"That old house was falling apart, even before the fire."

"Sure was."

Her husband grumbled, "It costs enough, even then." He looked down at the crowd with disgust.

"You hiring for construction?" a woman's voice rang out.

Lauren assured them, "Part of the construction agreement is they hire as much as they can locally. The factory is modular, so we can get started quickly and add to it as we go."

An excited chatter arose from everyone who had a cousin or uncle in the building industry.

Lauren said loudly, over the noise, "A whole new chapter is starting at Tisserande Linens and Megeso Point. Together, we're going to make our linens, our company and our town better than ever." She grinned, thinking of high school, and yelled, "Go Eagles!"

A huge cry went up, echoing her with their school cheer. Lauren felt tears in her eyes. Her husband looked at her, smirking at the effect the cheering had on her. She glared at him quickly, then glanced away. The factory build was out of his hands now. She knew she was doing the right thing, both for her and her hometown.

As the cheer died down, Lauren closed the meeting. "In the back of the room, besides doughnuts and coffee, we have a scale model and sketches of the new facility, so you can see where we'll be working next year."

With a flourish, the sheet was pulled off the model and people crowded around. The room roared with the excitement of the crowd realizing their town could thrive again.

2

Hotel Arrivals

Mia Spinel relaxed in one of the Adirondack chairs dotting the smooth green grass and looked out across the rich blue of the Atlantic Ocean. It was a glorious day, with just enough chill in the air to give her a reason for a cozy pink cashmere sweater and her cup of mulled cider. She'd walked around Moose Isle Inn this afternoon, exploring the hotel grounds thoroughly. Now, with her pink tennis shoes propped on the footrest, Mia gazed out at the breathtaking view spread before her. Moose Isle, a granite island emerging from the bay, was just tall enough to give a good view from almost anywhere, but the inn stood proudly at the top.

The Spinel Moose Isle Inn was a grand Gilded Age relic, a huge white clapboard building stretching up three stories, topped by a slate roof and a glassed in widow's walk. You could almost see the core of the house, even now, but large additions from ballrooms to guest rooms had sprouted from the main shell over the years. Lush green lawn, in defiance of the scanty Maine soil, carpeted the stretch between the main building and the shore, dotted with strategically placed balsam fir windbreaks.

On this side of the island, rocky cliffs stood high, guarding the island from the winter rage of the sea. The cliff tops were edged with pink beach roses, mixing their scent with salty iodine. The other side of the island sloped to a rocky beach full of pink granite balls. The hardy could swim in the chilly water in high summer, but the neighboring boat dock and fishing pier were more popular destinations. Most people preferred the glass enclosed heated pool off the hotel for actual swimming.

The hotel manager, Joesph Curry, casually strolled up, elegant as always in a Harris tweed jacket and wool trousers. "Enjoying your cider, Ms. Mia?"

Mia sipped the hot cider, inhaling the scent of rich apples and spices. "It's wonderful, Joesph. Everything looks great here."

"I'm glad. I never know what you'll tell me to fix on your first day here," he said sardonically. He sat in the neighboring chair and propped his feet up. Mia noticed his socks had tiny red lobsters decorating them, coordinating perfectly with a faint red line in his tweed jacket.

Joesph still cultivated a faint English accent, even after many years in the United States. Mia always found it amusing that the sophisticated man had chosen one of their more rustic hotels. He'd turned it into the Gilded Age splendor it was, a refined haven marooned on a wild

Maine island. He'd definitely borrowed from that bygone era's rusticators mentality. The hotel offered glorious daytime nature excursions around the island (always with appetizing picnic baskets in tow) followed by dinners worth waiting for. The winning combination drew guests, and kept them returning year after year.

"I know we have close to a full house," Mia said. Joesph nodded serene agreement. "But what guests do we have this week?"

"Only one wedding this weekend. It's still early in the season, but the bride wants a spring wedding," Joseph told her, his long, narrow face thoughtfully considering weekend plans. "It's a small affair, just thirty guests. Mostly family."

"I shouldn't say it as a hotel owner, but I think the more intimate weddings are usually the most fun."

"They're certainly the easiest to manage and keep everyone happy. This hotel definitely encourages the smaller weddings, with only sixty rooms." He waved his long fingers to encompass the hotel. "Lots of interesting activities for different age groups too. Hiking for the kids and elderly grandmothers can sit and watch the ocean." He smiled meaningfully at Mia.

Mia grinned back in mock disdain. "I'm not a grandma yet, thank you." She patted her smooth blonde hair. Not a gray hair showed—they wouldn't dare.

"Just a matter of time," he teased her, bony shoulders shaking in silent laughter.

Mia ignored him, looking out at the water. A new group seemed to be arriving.

"It makes for an exciting adventure, arriving on the boat. There's just something about an island." She loved watching new guests arriving. The Moose Isle Inn used a gorgeous Hinckley Picnic Boat for one of their hotel ferries. Wood and brass glowed in the orange tinged afternoon sun. The design was an elegant refinement of a lobster boat, riding all seas with graceful ease.

A woman lounged in the stern, arm draped casually across the back of the navy blue striped cushion, large dark sunglasses turned toward the setting sun, an excited smile on her face. A dark haired man sat across from her, laughing at something she'd said. On her other side, another man perched stiffly, not letting his body relax into the roll of the waves. A young woman clutched his arm, her spun sugar blonde hair spilling onto his jacket. Mia could almost hear her squeal as she jumped and clung to the older man whenever the spray might possibly touch her.

"Ah, the weekend's company junket has arrived," Joesph Curry told her. "The management of Tisserande Linens. You know, they used to make the best towels and sheets in the Northeast."

"It looks like a good group," Mia said. She peered with interest at the new arrivals. She'd have to get some bird watching binoculars to tuck in her bag. They would be so handy for closer observation. Only of birds, of course.

"The management is having their annual get together to congratulate themselves on record profits again, I'm assuming. A very successful company." He frowned, "It's rather odd they're coming here, you know.

The factory, well, just the company headquarters now, is up the coast a little, in Megeso Point. It's only a few towns away. I think they usually head to the Caribbean or somewhere."

"May in the Caribbean is beginning to heat up," Mia said. "It's much more pleasant weather here now."

"Yes, but I think winter is their usual time for their company affair. Winter's a better time to get away, around here. Who wants to wade through snow instead of walk on a sunny beach?" His face turned sharp, like a terrier on the scent. "I wonder why they're here now."

Mia smiled at his interest, "I expect we'll know by the end of the weekend."

"I expect we will." Joesph watched the group disembarking with focused attention.

As the boat docked, three men ducked out from the open cabin, two with drinks in hand. Douglas, the hotel harbor master, scowled at them, firmly removing their cut crystal glasses after they'd gulped the dregs.

Arriving in the boat was a perfect start to their stay, Mia thought, as she saw the happy face of the young woman tenderly helped off the boat by the man next to her. He smiled down at her, while helping the next passenger disembark safely. The woman laughed in delight as she pointed to one of the little sailboats ready for guests' use. He nodded enthusiastically, the two clearly planning a weekend sail.

The woman strode easily up the gentle slope of the island, leaving the group to follow her. Her wide pants rippled in the breeze, and her green sweater clung to her trim body. She moved like an athlete, long graceful strides making an easy journey up the hill. Laughing in pure joy, she pointed back to the mainland, Cadillac Mountain's pink granite glowing in the setting sun. "Isn't it beautiful?" she told Mia and anyone in earshot.

She paused to gather her group at the main entrance of the hotel. Only one other woman had kept up with her, the rest straggled behind.

The pale blonde woman's high heels caught on the rocks, making for awkward progress as she clung to the older man's arm. She apparently didn't think much of the rustic setting of the hotel, looking around her with disbelief. Her shocked, high pitched voice squeaked, "There's really nowhere to shop on the island? Why would anyone come here?"

The man informed her, "Oh, I think there are a few local shops in the village. Very arts and crafty."

The young woman made a face. "Not exactly my style, darling. Why couldn't we go to New York again this year? We live in Maine. Why do we have to vacation in this hell hole too?" Her perfectly fitted dressy pants suit, shiny silk blouse and expertly applied makeup agreed. The two continued their stilted progress up the rocky hill.

A woman with streaked spiky hair and orange framed glasses trudged by next. She was a little out of breath with a reddened face, even on the gentle slope. Her heron thin legs, clad in unfortunate orange pants, struggled to scale the hill, every joint clearly protesting her unusual spurt of activity.

Two men, who thought they were younger than they were, raced up to the hotel. Neither came out of it with flying colors. They collapsed on the green lawn in laughter, still breathing hard, as if running to the hotel was the funniest thing in the world.

A gawky man with big glasses lagged behind them, not joining in the race. He gazed around him with happy wonder, smiling at the hotel and waving a cheerful goodbye to the boat captain, who completely ignored him. He walked leisurely up the hill, stopping to admire his surroundings every other step, completely unconcerned about catching up with the others.

Very last to emerge from deep in the boat's interior was a well padded blonde in shiny candy pink with bright heels to match and a bloated whale of a man. He heaved himself out of the cabin, balancing carefully on the deck, his flesh quivering as he caught his balance. Wobbling, he cautiously stepped onto the dock, the boat rebounding visibly as it was relieved of his weight. He began his measured tread down the center of the dock, not bothering to look back at his companion.

The woman in pink waited a minute, clearly expecting the boat captain to help her on to the dock. He completely ignored her, ducking below.

Mia smiled a little, wondering how long it would take the woman to realize Douglas was not coming back on deck while he was alone with a woman on his boat.

Finally realizing the only way off the boat was on her own, she eased herself to the edge and jumped off, hampered only slightly by her spike heels. She lumbered up the hill, trying to catch up to the rest of the party.

Mia saw Douglas pop his head out of belowdecks, like a groundhog checking for safety. When he confirmed the passengers were well and truly off his boat, he ventured out with an obvious look of relief, making Mia smile.

The hotel concierge, a petite blonde vibrating with energy, came out to greet the scattered group. She expertly herded them, holding the door to encourage them to come inside. A bellboy hurried down the hill with a cart to gather the luggage Douglas was grudgingly offloading.

Joseph laughed softly after the little group entered the hotel. "That looks like a fun little junket. I'm glad I'm not the one trying to make them work together."

"Me too," Mia said, laughing. "I doubt they ever agree on anything. And I can't believe those two overaged boys ever work."

"I also agree with that young woman. This island is not exactly her style. New York would suit her much better."

"She's certainly not here by choice," Mia observed. "So that's the Tisserande group. Who else is here?"

"Mostly couples having romantic getaways. A few foodies making their pilgrimage to the fabulous Chef Ava. One or two family groups. Nothing out of the ordinary."

"That sounds like a good mix," Mia got up and stretched her arms out. "This island is always so relaxing."

She motioned to a happy older couple, a table between them heaped high with a glorious afternoon tea. The rotund man spread blueberry jam on a golden popover with gusto, his face avidly anticipating the treat.

"Your teas always look as delicious as they taste. It makes me feel like being lazy."

"You were climbing up and down cliffs all morning," Joesph reminded her. "I'm not surprised you're hungry." He pursed his lips. "You know Mark will kill me if you break an ankle. It's not just your life you're risking."

Mark Spinel, one of Mia's two stepsons, would definitely know who to blame if Mia broke something climbing on rocks. He'd blame Mia and berate her unmercifully, as usual. Not that it made a bit of difference.

Her stepsons and daughter adored Mia, but they much preferred her spending her energy organizing the Spinel family's hotels around the world, rather than home in Atlanta, organizing their personal lives. They actively encouraged Mia to travel as much as possible— and send back interesting presents.

"I'm looking forward to visiting the town tomorrow." The town proper was on the opposite end of the island from the hotel, a short brisk walk away. "Right now, I'm going to dress for dinner, and enjoy the hotel for a few minutes."

"Wonderful. I will see you later, then." Joesph made no move to go, gazing out to sea at the passing sailboats with calm interest, his long legs neatly crossed, polished leather brogues gently waving to his inner music.

Mia had never caught Joesph Curry doing any work whatsoever. He wandered around the hotel, gently gossiping, his elegantly lean body moving languidly, with all the time in the world at his disposal. She'd never actually spotted him in his wood paneled office.

Sometimes there were recent signs he'd been there, an open laptop, papers on the ornate antique desk, a still warm coffee cup. Never the actual man sitting in his office, doing anything as mundane as working. Joesph was strolling through the hotel, leisurely chatting with everyone. Nothing happened on the island without him knowing about it.

He was also one of the most efficient managers Spinel Hotels had. Joesph had organized several of their hotels around the world, and finally settled down here, on Moose Isle, when they'd first bought the property.

The hotel had been a decrepit, once grand house that had housed everything from a wartime convalescent hospital to a cult headquarters in its day. The only thing going for the aged wreck of an obsolete house when they'd first seen it was its sublime location in the Cranberry Islands of Maine, just off Mount Desert Island, with breathtaking views of Acadia National Park.

Mia and her late husband, Leo Spinel, had helped organize the complete renovation of the Gilded Age summer vacation "cottage." The beautiful structure of the immense white house was rescued, while the necessary ingredients for a luxury destination resort, such as the spa, meeting rooms and excellent bathrooms in every room, were added. Luckily, the original extravagant owners had planned their summer home to hold all of their hundred nearest and dearest in spacious rooms, so sixty guest rooms had easily been carved out of the hulk, with a few discrete additions.

Joesph had taken charge of the renovation. A magnificent hotel, like stepping back into another era, rose from the ruins. He'd flatly refused to take on any new projects, preferring to stay with his grand creation in rustic Maine. He lived in a charming cottage, designed by himself, on the hotel grounds, and seldom left his beloved island.

Mia loved coming here for two weeks a year, before the true Maine summer season started. She might suggest a few things to improve the hotel during her visit, but most of her time was spent simply enjoying the wonderful island and the season. Joesph always had the hotel in perfect order. She was on vacation.

The wide front porch held old fashioned white wicker chairs adorned with bright floral cushions and a view of the surrounding islands. An elderly lady with a froth of snow white hair and smile of eager anticipation perched, eying the silver tea tray placed on a table in front of her. A plate of blueberry scones waited temptingly, just in reach. Visibly giving in to an internal struggle, she smiled up at Mia, placing one on her plate, "I think I'd better get mine before my grandchildren get here. They've been hiking all day, and I think these delicious looking scones will disappear quickly."

"Absolutely." Mia remembered how fast dinner disappeared as soon as hungry children sat down.

The dark wood paneled hall inside was designed for grand entrances, with a curved staircase on either side of the large hallway leading into the main lobby. A chandelier dripped sparkling crystals from the ceiling, but most of the lighting was discretely ambient. She nodded in greeting to Kayla, the concierge, who immediately jumped up to see if she could possibly help Mia with anything.

"Can you make a reservation for tonight in the Acadia Dining Room?"

"I'll tell Chef Ava," Kayla said, bouncing with enthusiasm. "You have to try her clam chowdah. It's better than my mom's."

"I wouldn't tell your mom that. She might not make it for you any more," Mia told her with a smile, looking around the hall. "There aren't many people in the lobby right now?"

"Oh, everyone goes to the library, Ms. Mia. That's where we set out the nibbles." She consulted the huge grandfather clock ensconced in the corner. "People will start gathering there in about an hour."

"Thanks, Kayla. I'll just go and change for dinner, then." Mia headed for the elevators, surreptitiously tucked behind the grand stairway.

Her room was in the main building, one of the large older rooms surviving with its beautiful proportions intact. Her bathroom was carved off from the neighboring room. There were only two true suites at the Moose Isle Inn, with most of the large rooms arranged, like Mia's, into distinct bedroom and living room spaces.

The room felt airy and bright, with creamy white paneled walls catching the warm sunlight. Tall French doors lead to a balcony just big enough for two chairs and a tiny table, but with a magnificent view of the coast. A massive antique bed sat majestically on one side of the room, pale blue curtained drapes framing the tall four poster. Across the large room, a blue and gold Persian

rug framed a sofa and two comfortable chairs pulled up
to a tall fireplace. An exquisite watercolor of Cadillac
Mountain held pride of place above the fireplace. A little
sign hung next to it, "Pull for Fire Service," with an old
fashioned twisted pull rope beside it. Mia immediately
planned at least one evening with a cheerful fire and a
good book.

A bottle of champagne and a small cheese board
waited for her on the coffee table. She smiled at Joesph's
thoughtfulness and poured a glass of perfectly chilled
champagne. Sipping, she nibbled cheese and a cracker
and walked to the balcony, leaning on the railing.

From the balcony, she saw the whole of Southwest
Harbor in the distance. A lobster boat piled high with
traps was headed out to sea. A beautiful wooden yawl,
sails folded in the calm evening air, returned to the
harbor after a day spent sailing the Maine summer sea.
Tiny lights showed along Mount Desert Island's coast,
with just an occasional house light up higher on the
mountains. She tried to remember what the town in the
near distance was—maybe Northeast Harbor?

She remembered going to this house long ago with
her husband, Leo, wondering if they could possibly make
it into a hotel. The short boat ride here had been
miserable, gray and choppy. They hadn't been able to
climb the stairs to the third floor, so many of the boards
had been missing. They'd explored the property, planning
together, deciding whether the tattered remnant was
worth making into a hotel.

Leo hadn't been bald then. She smiled in fond
remembrance of his windblown hair standing straight

up. He'd looked like a mischievous round faced elf. She still missed him every day, even after two years. They'd had a wonderful life together. After the children were grown, they'd explored the world, living at all the Spinel Hotels in turn. They'd spend a few weeks or a few months perfecting each hotel, then move on to the next.

Mia tried to keep that spirit of adventure they'd enjoyed together, even now she traveled on her own. After all, you never knew what wonderful things the next day might bring.

The Moose Isle Inn had turned out even better than they'd expected, on that long ago windswept morning. Joesph deserved the credit for its transformation into a premier destination. And Chef Ava—her dinners were fabulous. Looking forward to tonight, she thought Moose Isle Inn was truly a hotel to savor. She sighed in pleasure, then suddenly sniffed sharply.

She definitely smelled smoke. Leaning out, she didn't see any bonfires on the grounds, but she did see smoke coming from a balcony at the other end of the wing. Mia quickly called Kayla, then hurried down the hall. One door had smoke oozing out from under the door frame. She knocked hard. "Is anyone in there? Is everything okay?"

A faint voice called back, "Everything's fine, just fine."

"There's smoke coming out of your room. You need to open this door right now." Several of the hospitality team ran up brandishing fire extinguishers, followed by Joesph strolling behind, massive red fire extinguisher casually swinging at his side. Even with modern fire prevention installed, fire was taken very seriously on an isolated island.

"Just a minute," and sounds of frantic activity behind the door. The door opened slowly and an innocent blue eye peeked out. "We're right in the middle of something. Can we get back to you?"

Mia demanded, "There is smoke billowing from your room. Open your door immediately."

To read more in
Mia's exciting next adventure,
please order

Ms Mia

and

Murder

on

Moose Isle

About the Author

J ennifer Branch weaves cozy mysteries with the vibrant flair of her watercolor paintings, inspired by her renown for capturing the Georgia coast. From her Northwest Georgia studio, she pens the Ms. Mia Murder Mysteries series, starring the charming champagne-sipping sleuth Ms. Mia, who solves murders in glamorous resorts. Her debut mystery, *Ms. Mia and Murder at the Grand Island Hotel*, sweeps readers to a Georgia Sea Islands paradise, followed by *Ms. Mia and Murder at Moose Isle Inn*, set on a Maine island.

As a modern impressionist painter, Jennifer infuses her stories with vivid settings, inspired by her artist's eye. When not writing or painting, she roams Georgia's salt marshes, coastal shores, and beyond with her husband, Roger, sons, Edwin and Owen, and dogs, Scout and Sam, finding inspiration in her travels. Visit Branchstudio.com to join her for more Ms. Mia adventures, books, and art!

Made in the USA
Columbia, SC
08 November 2025

72982397R00164